The Price of Loving a Hustla 2: Maliah and Case

By: Candace Lashell

For information contact; silverdynastypublications@yahoo.com

ISBN-13: 978-1542330909

ISBN-10: 1542330904

Dedication

This book is dedicated to all my supporters; I can't thank
each of you enough for all your kind words and
encouragement. It's because of you that the journey that I
am on feels so worth it. The support will never go
unnoticed or in vain. To Mercedes G. I'll forever be
grateful for you girl! Thank you for understanding my
vision. The ladies of SDP thank you! And Lexx Dymes a
special thanks to you, the push and love you give is greatly
appreciated. To my Love thank you for investing your time,
and helping to complete my vision. I'm forever grateful.
My beautiful babies, I just want to make you proud! Thank
you to all my family and friends; we can only go up from
here!

Follow me on

Instagram: Candacelashell

Facebook: Candace Lashell

Twitter: Candacelashell

The Price of Loving a Hustla 2: Maliah and Case

By: Candace Lashell

Recap:

I sat on a hospital bed for the second time in less than a month. Only this time, I was numb. I didn't feel an ounce of pain. All that I could envision was me frantically shaking Eriq's lifeless body to wake him up, but he never did. I had lost my mama and my child's father. The doctor held a light up to my eye, which caused me to blink.

Policemen filled the halls of the hospital waiting to question me on what I had witnessed. While all I wanted was to wake up from this nightmare, I couldn't help but to feel like I was still being punished for something cruel that I had done.

I replayed Eriq's conversation with me over and over again in my mind. *Gino, was behind hurting and killing my mama.* I thought.

"I have to go get my kids!" I snapped out of the depression I was drowning in.

"They are in the waiting area, Maliah." the doctor said to me.

"I need to see them. I need to hug them." I hopped off the bed and walked toward the door.

The doctor nodded to the nurse that it was okay to let me go. The guard escorted me to the area they were in. One of the police officers asked me if I was okay to give a statement, and I told him no. I didn't know anything besides Eriq was dead, and I'm sure they had that part figured out by now. I also knew that the hitter knew not to kill me. It didn't make sense. It was dark outside, but I saw them pause with hesitation and then they killed Eriq.

Eriq's story had some truth to it, and that was exactly why he had to die. He knew too much, and with my mama dead, they couldn't risk keeping him alive. I needed to talk to Case. He was the only person that could help me put this all together or even make me feel a little better other than the kids.

When I got to the waiting area, I was greeted by the children's tired, smiling faces. Marquita was sleeping in a chair, and Shawnie walked up to hug me.

"I had to go and get the kids because Mrs. Rice went down to the police station. Case was taken into custody for questioning on Eriq's murder," she whispered so the kids couldn't hear her. They had already been exposed to enough with the scene that she had just caused.

I stared in her eyes with tears welled up, and she nodded her head yes to give me confirmation of her words.

Was this the ultimate price I had to pay for loving a hustla?

Chapter 1: Maliah

I stood in the hospital lobby looking in the eyes of broken children. The eyes belonging to my sister, brother and son. They spent all night sitting in the hospital lobby not knowing what happened to me. I was hurt that they had to panic and await hearing from someone else if I was dead or alive. I was having trouble figuring that out myself. It felt like I was having a nightmare that I was never waking up from. On the verge of having a breakdown Shawnie embraced me with a hug not caring that I was covered with stains of blood. Right after she hugged me Mrs. Rice came storming into the waiting room like the true bitch that she was.

"Stay away from my god damn son. I'm not going to tell you anymore. This was the last straw, he ain't never been to jail, but here I am waiting on him to be given a bond because he's dealing with yo' ass."

I stared at her for a minute while I processed her words. It wasn't real that she was standing in my face talking about her son being in jail after I just witnessed Eriq being shot.

"Why would you even come here with this? And in front of the kids. You need to go home. You are in the wrong." Shawnie said to her.

"Shawnie you know I'm telling the truth. Our family didn't have these issues until she got involved." Mrs. Rice continued.

"Ma'am I'm going to have to ask you to leave." a police officer said to her.

"I'm leaving but you heard what I said Maliah, this is a warning to you." she walked off leaving everyone speechless at her lack of respect for me.

"Fuck her, Maliah. She's just a miserable old bitch." Shawnie said.

We sat down in some nearby chairs because my legs felt like they were going to give out from underneath me.

"It's going to be okay. We are going to make it through this, together." she said with her hands placed on my shoulders and nodding her head to reassure her words.

I heard every word she said to me clearly. I just could not find the words to respond to her. It felt surreal to witness Eriq get murdered right next to me. I couldn't get the last conversation we had out of my mind, the words kept replaying repeatedly.

"I would never hurt you purposely or kill your fuckin mama!" he shouted. "Mrs. Rice's husband is Gino." he said.

"Mrs. Rice?" I asked, looking at him with bewilderment.

"Yea, you heard me." he said, as I processed what he had just told me.

"He killed my mama?" I mumbled.

"My kids were at his house, while I was planning my mama's funeral." I was getting sick to my stomach.

"Come on, let's get out of here the kids are tired and hungry." Shawnie took Aden from Jaylen's arms and we all trailed behind her. It was good to be the presence of the kids. I wasn't sure if I was going to ever get to see their faces again after tonight's incident.

I kept saying a silent prayer that Casey was not behind the killing of my mama and Eriq. There would be no way I could live with myself knowing that I had been sleeping with the enemy all along. The kids all piled up in the back of Shawnie's Nissan as she drove in route to my house.

"I'm going to stay with y'all Maliah. I don't want you alone while grieving, or the kids for that matter." She added.

Once I was home I took a shower, where I broke down again watching Eriq's blood wash off my body and go down the drain. *Why am I not dead too?* I thought. It made no sense to me that the killer would pause and hesitate when he saw me, only to spare my life. Although he was masked I knew that it was not Casey behind the gun, the guy was too short for it to have been him. That did not make me want to rule him out though, and it also didn't mean that the killer didn't know who I was and knew not to kill me. I needed to talk to Casey and I needed to talk to him fast.

Shawnie and I sat on my bed talking about what I had witnessed that night. I purposely left out the information that Eriq had given me. I had been crossed by too many people, leaving me not to trust a soul.

"I don't understand why they have Casey in custody. Did Mrs. Rice give you any details when you went and got the kids?" I asked.

"I was home sleep when she called me panicking saying that Casey was locked up, and for me to come get the kids. I didn't ask her many details, because she was in a rush to get down to the precinct." Shawnie looked exhausted and I knew that she was tired of me asking her the same questions over. The sun was beginning to come up and we had still not been to sleep. We both lay down in my bed and proceeded to get some rest.

Just as I was getting ready to lay my head down Kayla was standing in the door way looking at me.

"Hey, you couldn't sleep?" I asked her.

"No, I can't sleep. This is just too much. You keep going to the hospital, and Casey done left the family." She said putting her fingers on her temples indicating that she was stressed out. I couldn't help but to smile even though the situation was far from funny. My little sister was growing up to be a little lady and I couldn't keep trying to fool them by telling them everything was fine when it was not.

"We are going to be okay, and you have nothing to worry about. I want you to go get some sleep and take your thoughts off of all of this."

Kayla walked back to her room rubbing her tired eyes. We all had been through more than enough and it was time for something to change.

I finally drifted off to sleep, but it did not last long, because I quickly woke up from a nightmare that had me in a cold sweat. The sound of gun shots was so vivid in my dream. I got out of bed to get my phone out of my purse. It had been dead since I called Shawnie to tell her to come get me from the hospital. I placed it on the charger in the kitchen and got a drink of water. I damn near dropped my glass at the sound of banging on my front door. I peeked out of my living room curtain and saw Casey's car in my drive way. I had so many unanswered questions and I could only get the answers from him. I opened the door and he barged in passed me like a mad man.

"Where is your phone?!" he yelled storming in my front door.

"You need to lower your fuckin' voice the kids are sleeping!" I snapped.

Shawnie came from the bedroom into the kitchen, rubbing her eyes.

Casey looked at Shawnie and then to me with a confused expression on his face.

"Step outside with me," he demanded.

I had on tiny pajama shorts, my hair was all over my head, and I didn't feel comfortable stepping outside with him. Shawnie must have sensed that I was not feeling his demand because she volunteered to go home and come back.

Casey wasted no time talking to me once she left.

"I spent all night worried, not knowing if you were dead," He said pacing the living room like he had for sure lost his mind.

"What were you doing in the car with him that time of night Maliah?!!!" he asked clearly not having any compassion for the fact that I had witnessed my child's father get killed. I was glad that he was asking these questions because it led right up to the ones that I had for ass.

"I met with him, only for me to find out you knew who killed my mother, and you had Eriq killed! You are mad that I could have fucked your hit up! That's the only reason yo' ass is here right now! You don't give a fuck about me! Then yo' old ass mama gone come to the hospital talking shit to me like I'm unworthy of *you*. When realistically none of y'all ain't shit." I yelled crying before throwing a candle holder that was on my counter toward his head. Casey ducked down in time for it miss him and hit the wall instead. He walked over to me and attempted to hold me, but I stepped back from is grasp.

"My mama came to the hospital?" he asked with his face screwed up.

"Yes, she brought her ass to the hospital and made it her business to try to blame me for your fuck ups!" I yelled finding myself getting more upset as the argument continued.

"Baby, I'm sorry you had to witness it and I'm sorry that your mama is gone. I had nothing to do with any of it. Yo' mama died from an overdose, Maliah. I don't know how many more times I have to tell you that shit," He said still attempting to grab my hand. I didn't want him touching me. I didn't even want him in my house or my life any more.

"They only took me into custody because they've been trying to pin me to all of this shit from the beginning, but I promise you I had nothing to do with any of it. I found out this morning that you were involved," He explained.

"Stop trying to fuckin touch me, Casey. I don't believe shit that you say! Get the fuck out of my house. If I had a gun on me I would blast yo' ass right now." I said crying and walking to my bedroom.

"You don't have to believe shit I say, but right now you need to pack yo' shit up because we are leaving." He had such a short temper that he could easily go from pleading with me to believe him to a *fuck this* attitude in an instant.

"I'm not packing nothing, or going no damn where with you," I said stopping in my tracks. If he thought that I was leaving to go somewhere with him he was sadly mistaken.

"I'm not asking you. These streets are hot right now and your name is all through shit since you were on the scene of the murder and so is mine. To protect you and the kids I must get y'all the fuck from out of Flint. Now!" he shouted. "You in here acting a damn fool and don't even know what the hell is going on. Yelling at me like you done lost yo' damn mind." He complained

Hearing him say the kids needed protecting sent me into a frenzy. I couldn't take any more pain, and if something happened to the kids it would for sure land me in jail or in a mental institution. I didn't get to pack much, because Casey was rushing me to move as fast as I could. I knew that when he said my name was in the streets he was referring to Eriq's brothers. It would be only a matter of time before they caught up with me for questioning and who knows what else.

I didn't want to trust Casey. I didn't want to trust anyone. I hated how much my soul followed his lead. A huge piece of me wanted to believe that he had no idea about the murders, but if his family was behind any of it there would never be a future with us. I was seeking vengeance and I would never ask him to stick by my side while I plotted on his parents. We cruised the expressway on our way to the airport. I had no idea where we were going. Casey didn't allow me to make a phone call to Shawnie before we left. He said no one could know that we were leaving. I felt horrible for not telling Shawnie what was going on after she had gone above and beyond to be there for me.

"I will tell you everything once we get to where we are going." He said breaking the thoughts of my guilty conscious. I nodded my head to him and continued to look out the window.

The one phone call that he did allow me to make was to Marquita. Before we went to the airport he made sure that we got her from school. Casey hated to pull her out, but he promised her that she would go back without missing a beat when we got to where ever we were heading to. Marquita wasn't happy with it but she understood the importance of our safety. *This is just some bullshit.* I thought

Chapter 2: Maliah

After flying an hour and a half we arrived at our destination; which was Boston, Massachusetts. To say I was pissed was an understatement. I had my heart set on some place tropical, and Boston was not a tropical place at all. I had been through so many life changing events in such a short period of time that I was having trouble remembering who I was, and Boston didn't seem like the ideal location for me recover from all of the trauma I'd experienced.

"Y'all are going to love it here for the moment," Casey said while removing our luggage off the conveyor belt in the airport terminal. You would have thought we were getting ready to have a family vacation of a life time the way that he was acting. He was being oblivious to the fact that we were there hiding out until we could resolve the issues we had back in our home town.

The kids all had long faces because they wanted to stay at their schools.

"I have to use the bathroom," I said.

This nigga had lost his rabbit ass mind bringing me to Boston.

As I walked away Aden began to cry while reaching out for me. My baby had lost his father and didn't even know it. Eriq and Aden had formed a bond in the short time that he was a part of his life and now he wouldn't even remember him. I went back and got my baby from Marquita. I located the airport restroom and went into a stall with Aden on my hip. I hung my purse on the hook and stood him next to the stall door. As I squatted over the toilet to pee he peeked under the stall at the anonymous woman next to us.

"Stop it boy." I scolded. He found it hilarious while doing it again.

"Aden, would you stop?" I hurried to finish to get him out of there. He was worse than a terrible two. The woman and I walked out of the stall at the same time. I had to take a double take at how beautiful she was. I was not a hater; and could never down play a pretty female. I had to give her props and this one was bad as fuck; from her pedicured toes on up to her flawless face.

She smiled at Aden. "You are too cute." He smiled back at her.

"You have your hands full. I can see he likes the ladies already," she said looking me up and down as if she was mesmerized.

"He is definitely a hand full." I responded while drying my hands. The way that she was looking at me made me uneasy.

While we were walking back to everyone Casey was talking to a man that was fine as hell. He was just as tall as him, light skin and had thick deep waves in his tapered haircut. I couldn't hear the words coming out of his mouth but I did see the full juicy pink lips from where the words were escaping. Casey said something funny to make him laugh and he displayed a perfect set of white teeth. *Fuck.* I thought while peeping how Marquita was eyeing him down too.

"Maliah, this is my brother, Nard." Casey said introducing us.

He didn't say anything to me for what felt like forever. I felt like I was under the eye of a hawk before it went in for the kill. Either the attraction between us was intense or his demeanor was strong. Whatever it was had me feeling uncomfortable and intimidated.

"Nice to meet you, Maliah." He finally uttered while extending his hand.

"Nice to meet you too." I shook his hand and quickly broke the trance he had me under. I didn't want to disrespect Casey, and I damn sure didn't want to stand there lusting or staring at his brother.

"I've been looking everywhere for y'all." The beautiful woman that was in the bathroom with us said.

"Hey everybody, and Mr. Peek-a-boo," she smiled to us, and Aden.

We all waved at her.

"This is my Assistant Aja." Nard introduced.

Assistant? I thought. I wasn't sure if that's how niggas introduced their girl in Boston.

I made a mental note of the way she was eyeing Casey too. I had a feeling Boston wasn't the move we should have been making.

"Well let's go. I got the trucks parked out front for y'all." Nard told us.

"Good lookin' Bro." Casey thanked him.

We drove in the back of the SUV for what felt like forever until we got to a beautiful house on Quincy Shore Dr. facing the Quincy Bay. The house was huge and so were all the houses around it. When the driver stopped, Casey wasted no time getting out to unload our bags. He unlocked the door and we walked in behind him. The house reminded me of the house that we were supposed to have moved into in Fenton, only the front view facing the bay was glorious. The kids ran through the house ecstatic. Marquita was even happy too and it was difficult to please her these days. She was creeping up on her 18th birthday and it wasn't much that I could tell her. She had become a know-it-all typical teenage girl, that constantly reminded me that I was her mother, despite me raising her.

Moving and getting us to safety was cool, but I wanted answers and I wanted them now. If Casey wasn't telling me the shit that I wanted to hear then I would be going to my own hideaway, and that didn't consist of him. I walked into the master bedroom and damn near hit the floor. It was as big as the whole house I was just living in, and the closet looked like another bedroom within itself. Casey came in behind me and closed the door. I was mesmerized by the bay window in the room that over looked the water outside. The sun was setting and it was a beautiful sight to see.

"So what happened, Casey? Why was I told Mr. Rice had my mama killed?"

He sat on the bed, rubbed his hands down his face and did an exaggerated sigh before answering my questions.

"Yo' mama stole some drugs from my pops. He ignored it and wrote it off as a lost, but Rosie was all over the hood bragging about it. I talked to my pops and told him to let it slide, and he did. Seriously Maliah she died from an OD."

Tears began to fall down my face. I knew that Casey always looked after my mama, but at that moment I didn't know what to believe, and I didn't like the feeling of being confused.

"Did your dad send that nigga to beat my mama the day she was attacked?" I asked in between tears rolling over my lips.

"I honestly don't know. I asked and was told no. I mean, that's all that I could go off."

To them she was just a crack head, but to me she was so much more. My mama stayed in a bunch of shit and people was coming for her left and right. No matter how much shit she was in, it would never change how I felt. I refused to let her death go in vain if it was a motive behind it.

"What about Eriq?" I asked hanging my head. I knew I had to go back to Flint to attend their funerals. Casey expressed that he didn't want us going back and that he was having my mama buried here in Boston. He kept stressing to me how unsafe it was for me to go back so soon, but I needed to say goodbye to Eriq. I visualized me holding his hand as he took his last breath, and chills crept up my spine.

"Naw, I didn't kill him, nor did I put the hit out on him." He said looking through his phone.

"You know who did it?" I knew that he knew who did it. Casey knew everything that went down.

"Naw." He responded still looking at his phone.

Casey had been focused on hunting Bridgette down to get Cailey, but no one had any information for him on her whereabouts, and he was going crazy. He couldn't put his phone down for two minutes.

"This bitch wants to play games with my baby." He said standing up and throwing his phone down on the bed. Our lives had changed drastically since we initially started our relationship. I honestly could not say that it was for the better. A knock on the door interrupted my regrets of being with Casey.

"Come in!" I yelled out. Before the words fully escaped my mouth, Kayla swung the door open causing it to hit the wall with a loud bang.

"Will y'all get him? He is getting on my nerve." She pouted while holding Aden who was crying at the top of his lungs and sliding down her leg. He was spoiled as hell, and no one wanted to deal with him. We were all responsible for his behavior, because everyone gave him what he wanted.

"You better stop all that crying!" Casey said to him. He immediately stopped crying and walked over to him and lifted his arms. Without any hesitation, Casey picked him up. Kayla stomped her feet and walked off. These kids and their attitudes were becoming too much.

"Well that was fuckin pointless. Telling him to stop crying only for you to cuddle him." I said shaking my head.

"We are going to dinner tonight as a family. I want to unwind with y'all." Casey announced. I had been through a traumatizing experience less than twenty-four hours ago the last thing that I wanted to do was eat at a restaurant. I was grieving the loss of my child's father, and Casey could care less. I had been through too much to still be the same caring, and understanding Maliah. That shit got me nowhere in life, because every time I turned around I was getting fucked over. The old me wouldn't have wanted to argue about us going out to dinner as a family, but that person no longer existed.

"I'm not going to eat no fuckin' dinner with you and *your* family when mine has been shredded to pieces. I don't know what type of shit you're on Case, but you have another thing coming if you think that I'm about to dine and have a good time with you after just witnessing my son's father die right next me. Not to mention my heart was already in a million pieces before that from my mama getting killed. You think I'm stupid enough to believe that she died of an overdose? I'm not fuckin with you, Case. Period." I vented. My thoughts and words were all over the place, and in my mind, he was to blame.

"I get it, and I'm sorry that I'm coming off as not being compassionate as you would like me to be. I only want to go out to eat because we *must* eat and I don't expect you to cook dinner for everyone. I can't fuckin' cook, nobody here but you can cook. So, unless you want to order a pizza, or I'll bring yo' ass some nachos while we all go out to dinner, all of us are going to a muthafuckin restaurant together…period." He said frustrated by how I was talking to him.

My stomach was growling. I hadn't eaten anything in over twenty-four hours and I hated to cave in but he was right. I was taking my ass to the restaurant. What I didn't want to do was eat no damn nachos or pizza while they were out enjoying steaks and lobsters because my pride had me trying to stand my ground. Casey got on my damn nerves, always making me contradict myself. I couldn't stand his black ass.

I didn't come here to live happily ever fuckin after. I thought

Chapter 3: Case

Last night was the worse night of my life. Hearing that Maliah was in the car during the night Eriq's bitch ass was clipped sent me into a rage that I had never felt before. The idea of something happening to her during a hit knowing that someway, somehow my family was affiliated, I wouldn't be able to live with myself. It kept fuckin with me the thought of her in his car that late. I wanted to know what were they talking about, and what were they doing. I hated the feeling of being insecure when it came to her. That's why more and more I wanted to depart from her. I had never been this venerable until the day I fell for her.

My heart went out to Maliah for losing her mama. I knew that more than anything, she wanted her mama to get clean and finally be the mother that she always wanted. Although I had nothing to do with Rosie dying, I still didn't want her to know about the attack on them coming from my pops directly. It was a relief that Rosie died from an overdose because that was one burden that I didn't have to carry on me.

I couldn't say that I felt the same remorse for Eriq. There was no man walking this earth that could ever say they jammed a gun to me and could live to tell the story. My mama told me that he was talking to people all over the hood asking them questions about our association to having Rosie touched. He knew too much about what was going, and it was only a matter of time before he told Maliah the full story.

When I was picked up after the shooting for questioning I knew that they couldn't hold me long. I was clean and they had nothing on me. It wouldn't be long before I met up with Gino to discuss the incident and get more details so that I wasn't in the dark about everything that had taken place. My first instinct was to make sure that their safety was not at risk while I tried to sort out the fact that our life was a big fuckin mess.

Selfishly I wanted to keep my name as clear as possible to her, because I knew that a future would never exist with us if I had to choose family over her. At some point that would have been the ultimatum and I was aware of my family's reasoning behind the attack. I desperately wanted to believe the streets that Rosie died from an overdose, because that was one burden that I didn't have to carry on me.

I stood there admiring her as she stood in the mirror curling her hair. She was just as beautiful as she was the day I first laid eyes on her. I couldn't help but to notice how thick her hips and ass were in her pants, or how beautiful her skin glowed under the lightening. *Damn, I was trippin' to have played her for Bridgette.* I thought. I tried to make sense of it every day and no answers came to mind at all. Maliah was the type of girl that niggas would only dream for in the hood, because amongst all the rats and thots, women like her didn't exist where I was from. You only had the Bridgette's.

It was crazy that I felt that Maliah wasn't fuckin' with me on that level anymore. She said her heart was set on doing what was best for her; whatever the fuck that meant. I was determined to put all this shit behind us and make her mine again. These days I was just hoping it was something that would pull us back together. Maliah needed to remember that I was that same nigga that she needed and wanted. The same one that tried to give her the best of everything.

I walked up behind her and pulled her in close to me so that she could feel how much I wanted her.

"What are you doing? Back the fuck up!" She snapped but still pressing her ass up against my dick.

"Stop playing. You know you don't want me to back up." She didn't say anything else, in-stead she held her head back and allowed me to trace kisses along her neck line. All I wanted was to make her happy and show her that it was a different way to live than what she was accustomed to. Unfortunately, life itself took that whole plan for a different spin.

I grabbed her hand and walked her over to the bed. All the time that she took getting ready I was about to make it all a waste. Before I had the chance to, she began removing her clothing piece by piece. That shit was a turn on seeing her just as eager as I was for it. She wasn't moving fast enough though, so I began to assist her in stripping quicker.

Once Maliah was fully naked I took a moment to take in her sexiness. She always shielded away from the attention I gave her, which added that sense of innocence to her style which drove a nigga wild.

I didn't want to waste any more time, because I was feigning for her. Nothing felt better than her tight wet grip. With ease, I laid her body down on the bed. I could feel how tense she was. I kissed her, to try to relieve some of the tension. Maliah never broke her eye contact with me, as I continued to work to get her aroused until I couldn't take anymore. I was ready to feel her. I parted her legs with mine and gently slide my dick inside her. She gasped for air and gripped the sheets as I continued to work into her.

"Yasss Casey," She moaned in my ear, as I continued to stroke her. With every stroke, she became wetter and wetter. Maliah nodded her head yes to indicate that I was hitting her spot. Once she gave me the confirmation I continued to attack it, until her body conformed to mine from her orgasm. It was no doubt that she was the best that I had ever had. I often found myself waking up in the middle of the night craving for her.

Sweat began to form over my body as I continued to pound away into her.

"Caseyyy I'm cumming." She informed me, making it my queue to join her on the trip to ecstasy. I collapsed on top of her wishing I could call off the dinner and sleep for the rest of the night. The sex was no different but her energy was off. I could feel that I was no longer the owner of her heart and that shit hurt. I had to get answers for her that would be substantial enough to clear my name, otherwise Maliah was gone and it wasn't no coming back.

~~~~~~~~~~~~~

We all gathered around the dinner table at the Atlantic Fish Company restaurant. Nard and Aja joined us for dinner. My baby brother had been living in Boston the past two years. It was on rare occasion that he traveled home to Michigan for anything. He had been successfully extorting drugs throughout the Jersey and New York area and felt comfortable residing in somewhere as low key as Massachusetts. Relocating my family here felt right since it had been working out for him for so many years, and despite what was going on with the rest of my family I trusted him. Nard didn't have kids, or a girlfriend, because for the most part he lived a fast-paced lifestyle that held no room for any of the above. He reminded me a lot of my dad in terms of his laid-back demeanor and serious personality. Although we were only step brothers, blood couldn't have made us any thicker.

"I appreciate y'all for inviting us out," Nard said taking a sip of his water.

"No problem. Thanks for joining us." I replied. I figured since we were all that we had in the city it was best that we all became acquainted. I could tell Maliah was not with us mentally at the restaurant. I knew that it would take time for her to process all the shit that happened and I was going to respect it.

During dinner, I took note of how Nard was checking for Maliah. In the past we had a history of passing off bitches to one another, but he was very aware that she was for sure off limits. Her beauty was undeniable so I never was insecure over a nigga checking her out, but I knew my bro and he always had to shoot his shot. The last thing I wanted to do was to cause friction between him and I over what was mine.

I also made note of how Marquita was checking for Nard. She was my little sister in my eyes and there was no way I would ever willingly allow her to mess with him. He was never known to have a healthy relationship with a female, or any relationship at all. Nard always got what he wanted from women and curved them afterwards. With all that was going on at the table, I was starting to believe that maybe moving here was not as good of an idea after all.

"So, what is it to do out here?" Jaylen asked Nard

"It's a lot man. There are tons of arcades, parks to hoop at, a nice mall to go get you some numbers at." He laughed and we joined in with him.

"Maliah, you've been so quiet and not said anything...is everything cool?" Aja asked.

"Yea, everything is cool. I'm just tired. Thanks for asking me." She responded without making any direct eye contact with her.

"Well, I'm happy to have you here. I can have someone to hang out with outside of Nard's up tight ass." Aja laughed taking a bite of her steak.

Maliah didn't respond to her comment. She simply smiled but still made no eye contact.

I never had to grieve the loss of a close loved one, but I was finding it very hard for me to remain cool while she was killing everyone's mood at the table.

"How long have you been in Boston?" Marquita asked Nard out of the blue.

Even he was caught off guard by her question. "I've been here a few years, not too long" he smiled at her.

Shit was beginning to get weird at the table, and it was time for us all to wrap the shit up. I wasn't feeling the fact that Aja kept purposely opening her legs so that her thigh would brush against my leg. She gave no fucks that Maliah was sitting right next me, instead she thought it would cool to talk to her about hanging out. Hoes were no good.

Later, that night after dinner Nard and Aja came over to our house to chill. I had one too many drinks at the restaurant trying to cope with the pain of not knowing where my baby girl was. Maliah decided to call it a night and get some rest. I told her I would put the kids to bed. I didn't have to put forth much effort into it because they were out cold on their own.

"Yo', how soon are you going back to Flint to handle that?" Nard asked me sparking his blunt. He was referring to Eriq's brother. I had a job to do and I couldn't have anyone with prices over my head let alone Maliah's. I was never the trigger man, but this was one job that I had to ensure was done correctly.

Aja fell asleep on the living room couch waiting on us to wrap up our conversation so I felt comfortable to talk to him about the situation. He freely spoke about too much around her and it made me uncomfortable. He tried to stress to me that she was the key piece to his organization, but the way I saw it bitches was always the downfall and he had put too much trust into this one.

"I want to make sure the family is settled before I dipped out, so prolly next week, but definitely as soon as possible." I nodded.

We continued to chop it up until the liquor and drugs took full effect over us. I wanted to go slide in the bed and hold Maliah, because I was sure that she wasn't sleeping good.

"Nigga, my head is spinning, I'm about to chill here for little while." He said removing his snap back and lying back on the couch.

"Yea I was going to say nigga, you've been drinking too much to drive," I said agreeing to his decision.

I somehow made it up the staircase into our bedroom. The only light in the room was seeping from under the closed door in the bathroom. I slide under the covers and embraced Maliah's smooth body. I planned to make every wrong with her right, even if I had to die doing so.

Chapter 4: Maliah

"Mmmm Casey," I moaned as I snugged my head back deeper into the goose down pillow. I was in ecstasy. It wasn't until I heard him snoring loudly next to me that I realized it wasn't him doing the pleasuring underneath the covers. I was having a hard time figuring out why I couldn't stop my toes from curling and I was being awakened out of sleep by oral pleasure. The feeling was so intense that I was terrified that I was locked down to the bed, afraid to make a move because I didn't want the feeling to end. I had never felt this good from receiving head alone. As my body began to reach its peak the mysterious person added more pressure to throbbing clit.

My back arched off the bed and I gripped the sheets as tight as I could. All that I could do at this point was embrace the climax that was about to take over my body.

"Ohh shiiittt!" I cried bucking my hips.

While I was coming down from the intense feeling Aja's face came from under the sheets.

"What the fuck are you doing?" I whispered to her not wanted to wake Casey. I was embarrassed that this had just happened.

"Oh my God, I'm so sorry. I was drinking and… I'm so sorry, Maliah." She whispered back to me.

This bitch wasn't sorry. You don't accidently roam through someone's house, walk into their bedroom, climb in their bed and begin eating pussy. I was two seconds from whooping her ass. I had never been so violated in my entire life.

"Get the fuck out of here now," I said just above a whisper this time. Casey's drunk ass wasn't waking up.

"I really am sorry. We don't have to mention this ever again," She said standing up.

I wasn't in Boston a good twenty-four hours and I had already been raped. The fact that Aja had done such a great job pleasing me, I didn't know whether to be mad at her or to kiss her. I watched her rush out of the room as I sat up on the bed. *Did that just happen?* I thought. My life was beginning to be all too much.

"Casey! Wake yo' ass up!" I yelled while nudging him.

"What?" he groaned peeking out the corner of his eye

I snatched the covers off him, not caring about him being comfortable.

"What?" he repeated, this time with an attitude.

"Get me the fuck out of this house, now! I'm two seconds from going to jail. I just woke up to Aja eating my cookie. I'm not dealing with this type of shit in my home." I was not telling him that I enjoyed it. This was about the principle.

"You woke up to what?" He was now more alert, even though his eyes were still closed.

I refused to repeat what I had just said because I felt like he was asking me to repeat myself on purpose.

"You heard what the fuck I said, now get me away from these sick ass people you have in this house." I didn't know a thing about Nard or Aja and he had them wondering through the house while the kids were here.

"I heard you. Did you like it? Did she do a better job than what I do?" He asked chuckling. It wouldn't have been Casey if he wasn't making a joke out of it.

"The shit is not funny. She blamed it on the alcohol, but you and I both know that she's lying." I huffed

"I know you, and you ain't that mad about it. But I'm about to go see what is up." He laid there for a minute before sitting up. "For real, though, did she do a better job than me?" he asked laughing hysterically.

I threw the pillow at his head. I was frustrated because she did do a better job and he found this situation to be so funny.

I never would have thought that I could be violated in such away and enjoy it. Now I had to be around this hoe unsure of how I felt about her. *Shit is getting so crazy.* I thought.

Chapter 5: Marquita

I sat in my room texting my girl Tiffany from school back in Detroit. Case made it clear not to tell anyone where we were and I was abiding by that. It didn't stop me from thinking this was some straight bullshit that I was stuck in Boston two weeks before my 18th birthday. I stood in the mirror admiring my body. I had been putting in time at the gym and it was showing in all of the right places.

The move didn't sit well with me but I had to admit that this house was nice. I couldn't believe we went from a little ass two-bedroom townhouse to a huge ass mansion off the bay. I was so appreciative of Case and all that he had done and was willing to do for us in the future.

I decided to roam the house and get familiar with where everything was. The long hallway upstairs was where all of bedrooms were. There was another room on the main floor, but Case had it set up as an office. As I made it to the main floor I couldn't help but to admire the beautiful staircase. I felt lost the second I got down the steps, because of the several hallways leading to all same rooms. Rather than turn around I continued to wander. I opened a door that was close to the kitchen and was greeted by Nard's fine ass as he slept on the couch.

I never had a hard time with blowing niggas off, hell, I was still a virgin. As far as I was concerned none of the niggas that I had come across were worthy of having me. I took a second to enjoy the sight of him in front of me before I decided to leave. It was like he had a sixth sense, because before I got a chance to walk away, he opened his eyes and looked dead at me. To say that I was embarrassed wouldn't have been saying enough. I was caught red handed watching him sleep. I stood there like a kid caught with their hand in the cookie jar.

"Why are you standing over me?" he asked trying to adjust his eyes after abruptly waking up.

"I *was* trying to figure out who was sleep down here in my house." I lied. I couldn't let him think that I was watching him.

I turned around quickly to leave the room and go have a long talk with myself about what had just happened.

"Where you going?" he asked rearranging the heavy linked chains that hung from his neck.

"Back to my room," I told him still making my way out the doorway.

"You can stay in here and chill with me." He suggested. As bad as I wanted to take him up on his offer I couldn't. I didn't want to get caught by Case or Maliah chilling with him.

"Naw, I'm good. I'm tired." I told him while fake yawning.

"What you afraid yo' sista gone catch you chillin'?" he asked reading my mind.

"No, I just told you that I'm tired." I was offended that he was making me out to be a kid.

"Alright, good night then," He said laying back down.

"Night," I mumbled deeply wanting to stay. I took one more peek at him before leaving and closing the door behind me.

Why is he so damn fine? Having him around was going to be tempting and I wasn't sure if I would be able to keep declining him on his offers if they continued. Rather than trail off to my bedroom I decided to go in the kitchen for a glass of juice. My thoughts drifted off to me wanting to do something nice for my sister. She had been through a lot in the last past year and I wanted to give her something to show my empathy and appreciation.

"I thought you were going to bed?" Nard asked me breaking my thoughts.

"I'm about to now, I thought *you* were going back to sleep" I responded. He opened the refrigerator door to retrieve a bottle of water. He wasted no time opening it and guzzling it down.

"Sheesh, slow down before you choke on the water." I chuckled.

"All that liquor got me dehydrated as fuck." He said while shaking his head.

"How old are you, Marquita?" That question came from left field.

"I'll be eighteen in a few weeks, why?" I frowned

"Cuz I ain't tryin' to be locked up for messing with yo' young pretty ass." Nard laughed.

Messing with me? It hadn't been twenty-four hours since we first met so I was confused on where all this was coming from.

"I'm an adult, and you aren't *messing* with me. You have a girl. I want no parts."

I was far from stupid I saw past his boss/assistant relationship with Aja. Their body language told that they were very comfortable in each other's personal space, and I didn't like the idea of him being Case's brother. I had never dated anyone seriously because I usually became bored very easily.

"Man... chill out" Nard said walking toward my direction. I guess the alcohol still had him consumed because he was being very bold with his actions.

"You ain't tryin' to go there?" He asked now standing well within my comfort zone.

"No. Not only am I not about to be messy with you, but I don't even know you!" I snapped on him.

"That's what I'm asking, for you to get to know me. I ain't asking you to be messy. If you're doing what you are supposed to you won't have to worry about the next female." He was now so close to me I could feel his breath blow past my face.

"What I'm *supposed* to? What exactly does that mean?" I asked crossing my arms interested in hearing the next piece of bullshit to his game.

Nard didn't say anything, he instead leaned in to kiss me. I wanted to slap him for thinking that was acceptable behavior. I stuck my hand out to stop him before he started. This seemed to have been usual behavior for him and alcohol wasn't to blame. He looked at me as if I had grown two heads. Apparently, he was very unfamiliar with rejection.

"You tried it. I like my niggas to be exclusive and you rub me as the type that keeps them lined up," I said judging him

The smirk that he possessed told me that he was feeling my attitude. Dudes like him thought women came a dime a dozen and I was going to be the first to let him know that I wasn't for the games.

"Alright, have it yo' way." He made it seem like I was missing out on something when him and I both knew that he wasn't hitting on shit when it came to building relations. I walked out of the kitchen no longer caring to talk to him. This was what I meant by I became bored. Nard was fine as hell but I wasn't feeling his demeanor one bit.

"So, you really ain't fuckin with me?" He asked in shock.

Without acknowledging his question, I continued to leave the kitchen.

This nigga is foolish. I thought

As I walked down the hallway I bumped in Aja coming out of the bathroom. She looked like she had seen a ghost.

"Hey, what are you doing up so late?" she asked.

Aja was very pretty, but because I silently was crushing on Nard I was being a hater telling myself that she was ugly. Whatever type of relationship he had with her was a close one. They watched each other's next step, and the way they moved was in unison. I had picked up on that the entire night and it made me uncomfortable. She opposed as a threat of me getting to know him. It made me wonder what his profession was that required the use of an assistant that was around even during non-business hours.

"I couldn't sleep so I was just up chillin' with Nard." I said purposely hoping that it would bother her.

"Oh…is he awake?" she asked showing signs that my comment had gotten to her.

"He's in the kitchen," I said continuing to walk down the hall toward my room.

This new living situation was getting to be very interesting and I was ready to see how it was going to all play out.

Chapter 6: Maliah

I stood outside on our deck as Casey introduced to me Ms. James. She would be our new nanny. I was not feeling the idea of having some strange woman helping me with the kids. I would much rather go back to Michigan and face the conflict that was awaiting me there. Three weeks of us being in Boston had gone by and I was home sick. The air didn't even smell the same, the people were weird to me and I didn't like the feeling of not knowing what was going on back at home.

We had my mama's ceremony held here, as well as got her cremated. Since we had no immediate family it wasn't much of an argument on where her body was taken. I still pressed Casey on Mr. Rice's connection to my mama's death, but he kept deading the subject and promising me there was no connection.

"Hi Maliah, I've heard great things about you. It is a pleasure to meet you" The older mocha brown lady said extending her hand.

"Nice to meet you too." I shook her hand and cracked a half smile.

"I know how difficult it is as a mother to have a stranger come in and care for you, but I helped in raising Case and his brothers, and they turned out pretty decent." She laughed.

"Oh Lord. I don't know about that one," I countered laughing with her

"Y'all got jokes I see." Casey frowned.

"Let me get started on preparing dinner." Ms. James said walking toward the patio door.

"Make it light Ms. James, Maliah and I have a date tonight." Casey announced. A date was news to me. He hadn't mentioned any of these plans to me.

After Ms. James went into the house I couldn't wait to ask him about what he'd claimed.

"When were you going to inform me that we had plans tonight?" I asked him with an attitude.

"It was going to be a surprise but that ain't go well. I want to take you out, because Nard and I are going to Detroit in a couple of days to tie up some business."

He was still dropping news on me. I wasn't stupid I knew that he was going back to Flint on some bullshit. He probably was trying to sweep his dirt under the rug. I was far from stupid and little did he know I was going to be the investigator from hell. As bad as he wanted to forget all of my allegations, it was just as bad as I wanted to know the truth. If Casey wanted to be untruthful to me then he gave me no option but to get the answers I need behind his back. My plan was in full motion and I was gearing up for the drama that I knew was about to head our way.

I also had to sit and have a talk with Ms. James. I was apprehensive about leaving a stranger home with the kids while we both left.

She stood in the kitchen with her head buried into the cabinet looking through all of the seasonings to begin dinner.

"So, how long have you been here in Boston?" I asked observing her physical appearance. She looked like the sweet Grandmother that I never had. That didn't mean much to me though because I understood that looks could be deceiving.

"I've been here for a little over a year now. I was staying with Nard when Casey asked me to come over here and give you guys a helping hand," She said standing at the sink filling a pot with water.

"So where is your family? Why did you choose to stay around them over being with your relatives?" I needed to know why she was a loner and made a living working to take care of someone else's family.

"My husband died from lung cancer six years ago, and I lost my daughter four years after that," she replied turning to look at me.

"I'm so sorry to hear that. If you don't mind me asking, what happened to your daughter?" I felt bad for asking but I felt like I needed to know.

Ms. James took a long pause as she gathered her thoughts, and emotions before she spoke.

"You remind me a lot of my daughter with these questions, your beautiful face and good spirit. Her name was Alyssa, she was smart, driven and had a huge giving heart. She was in love with a guy that was no good for her. He was in the streets and lived by the gun. No matter how many times I told her to stay away from him she didn't listen. In fact, it only drew her closer to him. Well, one night she was riding around the city with him when his car was shot up forty-six times. My Alyssa was in the car." Ms. James began to cry hysterically.

"She was all that I had left and I failed at protecting my baby. She was only twenty years old." She continuing to cry.

I walked over to embrace her with a hug. It broke my heart hearing her story and thinking about my own life.

"I'm so sorry." I managed to say.

"It's okay, it will always be hard for me to talk about." Ms. James began to dry her eyes with a piece of paper towel.

"Just take my story as a lesson. I see you have your hands full here. Don't let your life go past caring, and worrying about pleasing others," She said hugging me.

I allowed her words penetrate my mind. She gave me the feeling that she genuinely had my best interest at heart.

~~~~~~~~~~~~

Dinner was silent. Casey and I didn't do much talking amongst each other. I was still psychically attracted to everything about him, but it was going to take more than a psychical attraction to get me back in love with him. I missed the way we were before all the drama happened in our lives. If I could forget any of this happened to go back to when he first walked up to me in the diner I would with no hesitation. I watched Casey as he took a bite of his Cajun Alfredo. Every time he would chew his dimples were visible. His eyelashes were so long that you couldn't help but to notice them as he looked down into his plate. The sight of him was enough to make any woman smile. I shied away from admiring his gorgeous appearance as he looked up at me.

"So what's on your mind, Maliah? Talk to me." Casey said trying to make eye contact with me, but I wasn't having it. Every chance I got I wanted him to know that he was not in my good graces.

"Nothing besides I want to go home, but you already knew that," I countered sarcastically.

He became annoyed with me the moment the words escaped my mouth. I was frustrated I couldn't attend Eriq's funeral, which made me even more suspect and public enemy #1 back home. I had been talking to Shawnie on Facebook behind Casey's back and she told me that word on the street was I had Eriq set up the night he got killed. It fucked me up that people thought that I was cold enough to have something like that done to him. We had our differences but I didn't have a reason to hate Eriq enough to want him dead. We were doing a great job at co-parenting Aden. I would never have my son's father set up. It just wasn't my character, regardless of what anyone thought.

I wanted nothing more than to clear my name. I was just as clueless as everyone else as to why I wasn't killed with him.

"I don't know why you ask me what's on my mind and then you fuckin ignore me when I tell you." I was tired of his nonchalant attitude toward me losing my mama and Eriq.

"I didn't bring you here for this shit. I'm trying to make you happy and take your mind off it all." He tossed the napkin he used to wipe his mouth with on the table.

"If you want to make me happy then you would take me back home and let me straighten out all the lies being told Casey," I said on the verge of tears.

"Ain't no straightening shit out! You so damn naïve man, those niggas don't want to hear yo' side of the story. They want you dead, and it's up to me to protect you. That's my job Maliah, rather if you want to believe it or not that's on you." The vein that throbbed in his forehead when he was angry was out. "I'm not going to keep explaining this shit to you, and I'm not going to keep telling that you ain't going home," he said with venom in his voice.

I felt like a defeated child being told no by their parent. Casey had no right to tell me where I could or couldn't go. I was only here in the first place because I acted without thinking when he said that the kids weren't safe.

I got up and went into the restroom of the restaurant to cool myself down. I wanted to argue with him so he could understand this from my perceptive, but I knew that was a dead cause. As I regrouped myself I sat on the bench that was in the rest area and checked Facebook to see if I had a message from Shawnie. I missed her like crazy, and besides the kids she was the only thing keeping me sane. I hadn't told her where we were located but I talked to her daily. Now in my inbox, I saw that I had no recent messages from Shawnie and I instantly became sad.

As I filtered through my messages I came across one from someone that had no profile picture of themselves, but one of a spiritual quote. What caught my attention was the mentioning of baby Cailey. I opened the message and it read:

Hello Maliah, my name is Mrs. Patterson. Can you please call me? It's about Baby Cailey. Please don't tell Case that I am reaching out to you. 847-778-9878

I began to panic thinking that something may have had happened to Cailey. Fear set in as I left the rest room in search of my table to get back to Casey. The person asked me not to tell him, but seeing how sick he was behind his daughter being missing I wanted him to know that I had a possible lead. As my thoughts took over I had to pause; I needed to call the woman first to see what she had to say and who she was before I told him. It had to be a reason behind her not wanting me to tell him. My plan was to call her and then let Casey know what was going on. He always acted on impulse and if Cailey was in danger he would not think the situation through.

"You got lost in there?" he asked sarcastically.

I smirked at him. I never gave into slick ass remarks that would have made it too easy for him.

We ate dinner and continued to make dry small talk the remainder of the night. The whole time I had thoughts of the baby on my mind. I needed to get Casey from around me so that I could call the number.

"How about this… we get a room tonight and I knock some happiness into you." He smiled displaying his dimple.

His words caught me off guard and I couldn't help but to laugh.

"That won't make me happy," I said still laughing.

"You wanna bet?" He asked in a more serious tone.

I wanted to take him up on his offer but I needed to get this call in, so I had to think of something quick.

"Drinking all of this water has me using the restroom every minute. I have to go again, if you'd excuse me." I scurried off before he had an opportunity to ask me anymore questions.

I was going to call the number from my inbox and see what the hell was going on. As soon as I hit the restroom I wasted no time. The phone seemed to ring forever before an older lady answered.

"Hello?" The voice of a woman crackled on the other end.

"Hi my name is Maliah and I was instructed to call this number," I said probably too fast for the lady to grasp.

"Maliah, this is Mrs. Patterson, Bridgette's mother. I reached out to you because I have Cailey here with me. She's been here since last week, and I can't properly care for her. I am sick with cancer. Bridgette has been neglectful, and worried about everything but my granddaughter. Cailey needs to be with her father, until Bridgette gets it together."

I wasn't shocked by anything that Mrs. Patterson was telling me. Bridgette wanted Cailey for all the wrong reasons, and that was the hopes of keeping Casey around.

"Okay, I can come and get her. She can most definitely come to live with us. Can you please inbox me you address? I will come get her as soon as possible." I was hesitant to believe anything that she was saying because for all I knew it could be a setup. Bridgette could not be trusted and who was to say her mama could be either.

"I sure will. Hopefully Bridgette gets it together soon. She's so busy worried about the two of you that she is losing her mind. I would appreciate if you didn't bring Case because the last time he came here he caused me all kinds of stress, even after I told him I hadn't seen Bridgette in months." She complained about Casey's crazy tactics.

I was curious to know how her mother knew who I was or how to search for me on Facebook, but I figured Bridgette had told her enough about me, so it wasn't hard.

"T you, Mrs. Patterson for contacting me. I will see you soon." I couldn't make her any promises on not bringing Casey. It would be impossible for me to make it Illinois without him hot on my ass.

When I walked out of the restroom Casey was standing right by the door scaring the shit out of me.

"What is wrong with you? I don't need you waiting for me by the door," I snapped rolling my eyes.

"You on some sneaky bullshit and I'm not feeling it," he affirmed with a toothpick hanging from his mouth.

"Ain't nobody being sneaky. I was using the damn bathroom Casey." I lied.

"I don't like being *lied* to Maliah, and you ain't even good at it."

I told Casey everything that just happened, without sparing him any details. I didn't care about the fact that he would be upset that I was on Facebook, because the outcome of it was us being reunited with Cailey. His plans on us going to a room were over for, and we were on the next thing smoking from Boston to Illinois.

Chapter 7: Marquita

I didn't know how many more boring ass days I could take it in this state. I was slowly on the verge of contemplating suicide. I sat on the floor in the hallway playing UNO with Kayla. She had become my best and only friend over the past month.

"Uno!" she shouted for the fifth time that night.

"Okay, that's it. I'm done. It's time for you to go to bed." I told her putting the cards back in the box.

Our new nanny had taken off for the evening and I was ready to call it a night myself. I peeked in Aden's bedroom and he was sound asleep, while Jaylen was in his bedroom playing on his X-Box One. Maliah called and instructed me not to wait up for them and that she would be back sometime tomorrow. I was excited that she had gotten out of the house. I had hopes that Casey did something nice and romantic for her. She had not been herself these last couple of days and I was beginning to worry about her.

As I got settled in my bed, the land line rang. No one ever used that phone unless we had a visitor and the gate needed to be opened. I turned on my TV to view the video from the camera footage that Casey had set up in the house. I Saw Nard's sexy ass hanging out his car window pressing the intercom button. I authorized for the gate to open and I met him at our door. I was wondering if Casey sent him to check in on us since they were gone overnight.

He was shocked to see me answer the door.

"Where is Case? His phone is going straight to voicemail."

"Hello to you too with yo' rude ass. He ain't here and I don't know where he is." I proceeded to slam the door in his face.

Nard prevented the door from slamming with his arm. He was lucky he was cute because otherwise I would have taken his arm off in the door.

"My bad. I'm a lil on the edge and need to talk to him." He apologized.

"He will be back tomorrow," I huffed noticing the stress he seemed to be under.

"Come chill and smoke an L with me in my car." He suggested.

I didn't smoke but I was bored as hell and didn't mind taking him up on his offer to chill. Jaylen was still up just in case Kayla or Aden woke up.

We sat in his Jaguar XE. The car matched him; it was smooth and but not too flashy, a lot like him.

"So you got a lil boyfriend back home?" He asked rolling up a blunt.

"Naw, I don't have a *lil* boyfriend. I'm too busy focused on school."

"What are you going to school for?" He questioned after sealing the blunt with his tongue

"Mortuary science." I murmured.

"Dope, we can become a duo. After I'm done with the bodies you can dispose of them." He said with a straight face.

Was that a joke? What kind of sick shit is that to say?

"I'm straight. I don't want to assist you with your dirty work." I didn't know what his occupation was but I was almost sure he was a street nigga.

"I'm kidding, it was a joke." He smiled

"I thought jokes were meant to be funny." I sneered

"So what you like to do for fun?" he asked while sparking the lighter.

I knew that this conversation was going to come soon from him. Nard was a dog and he didn't hide the signs either. He was very straight forward with what he wanted and how he wanted it.

"I like to draw," I answered dryly. He wasn't interested in me or what I had going on; he wanted one thing and one thing only. So, me sitting up here telling him that I was interested in art was the real joke.

"Word? I love art. Maybe when you have time you can draw me a picture." He responded with low eyes.

The smell of the smoke was causing me to cough. I had never smoked a day in my life. After seeing my mama on drugs all my life I did not want any parts of it. A natural high is what I would be off. Nard put the blunt out in consideration of me damn near choking to death.

"I take it you don't smoke," He said

I shook my head no still trying to catch my breath. He pated my back and stroked it to help soothe my cough.

"You good?" He seemed to be concerned with me struggling to regain my composure.

"Yea I'm fine." He placed his hand on my thigh. I looked over at him and he smiled at me with low eyes.

"I want you Marquita, fa real," he told me looking down at his hand on my leg.

I wanted him too, but our wants I'm sure were different. I wanted to see what he was about, and give him the benefit of a doubt. He attempted to kiss me again, only this time I didn't stop him. This was not my first time making out, but it was a lot different than what I was used to. Everything was moving fast and aggressive. He ran his hand up and down my thigh never letting me up for air. I was too caught up in his frenzy to stop him. Finally, he broke our kiss to breathe.

My head was spinning, I was dizzy as fuck, and unsure of what had just happened. He reached over me and began to let my seat back. The beating of my heart felt like it was about to explode out of my chest. Once he had the passenger seat back as far as it could go he looked at me asked, "Are you sure?"

I wasn't *sure*. I didn't know why he was asking me if I was *sure*, I didn't know how I had gotten myself in this situation and I was at a lost because sex was something that I had never had before. My ideal first time was not going to be in the passenger seat of a car.

"Wait, no. I'm not feeling this," I responded smoothing my hair down with my hand trying to get myself together. Nard immediately gave me the space that I needed by sitting up in the driver's seat.

"It's cool. I don't want you to be uncomfortable." He said

I was very uncomfortable and overthinking what could happen if I followed through with sleeping with him. I didn't want to fuck in his car in front of *my* house. My heart dropped to the floor as a car pulled in front of us with the headlights beaming nearly blinding me. I just knew that I was about to be caught in the care with home and smelling like weed. I tried to think of something to tell my sister so she would think nothing of me chilling in the car with him.

"Fuck," I mumbled under my breath.

The lights went out on the car and it wasn't Maliah and Casey......it was Aja.

She got out of the car wearing some little shorts and a cut off shirt. She slammed the door of her Ashton Martin and walked towards the car we were in. Nard remained cool, while I was furious that I didn't secure the gate after letting him in, and this hoe was ruining my moment. He didn't open the door or let the window down; leaving her to stand there looking stupid.

"Why is she here? Especially if you claim she isn't your girl. I don't know any females that pull up on a man that ain't hers, and she looks pretty pissed off to me," I was annoyed by her presence. I was not about to deal with her every time I wanted to get close to him.

"She's not my girl, she just has attachment issues," He shook his head out of frustration.

"Attachment issues? Nigga, who do you think you're talking to? You need to handle your business and leave my presence." I huffed.

He let the window down to hear what she had to say. Aja stood there saying nothing with her arms crossed.

"What?!" he yelled in annoyance.

"Why are you here Nard? Casey doesn't appear to be here, so why are you here?" she questioned him

"Go home, Aja. You know I don't like you looking for me and I don't like you questioning me." he said in a calm tone

"I don't give a fuck what you like! You sitting out here with this young ass girl and you've been blowing me off all day."

Nard, open the door to step out the car.

"Young ass girl?" I repeated. She didn't know who she was talking to. I would beat the shit out of her and not think twice about it. Fighting was my specialty and she had no idea the ass whooping that she was signing herself up for.

He turned around and looked at me and without him even opening his mouth I knew to shut the fuck up. He has a presence about him that you just knew not to step out of place of the consequences would be heavy for all parties.

He grabbed her by her arm aggressively causing her to wince in the pain and then forcefully walked her back to her car still holding on to her arm. Tears ran down her face as he pushed her down into her car. I couldn't hear what he said to her but she got the fuck on with no hesitation. That should have been my queue to do the same and follow her lead. A man should never handle a woman as aggressive as I had just witnessed him do.

Nard got back into the car as if nothing had happened letting me know this was normal behavior for him and her.

"I'm about to get some sleep," I said yawning. I was tired so it was the perfect excuse to escape his crazy ass.

"Don't let her ruin what we were doing. I would never treat *you* that way. She just gets besides herself invading my personal life," He looked into my eyes forcing me to believe the words he was saying to me.

The stupid side of me felt special hearing him refer to me being a part of his personal life. He leaned in to kiss me again and I let him. He smelled so good and his lips felt good against mine. I felt like I was older and dealing with a nigga in the big leagues, and I loved it.

"Come on," I led him to the front door after we got out of the car. This was about to be the most action I've had since I got to

Boston. Nard followed me through the house and up to my room. I was certain to make sure that Jaylen didn't see us creep past his room, because he would for sure snitch on my ass.

I closed and locked the door behind me, and turned the lights off. The only light in the room was from the moon that peeked into the window.

"Turn the lights back on. I want to see you." His words caused me to rethink my decision. I was inexperienced and had never had sex a day in my life. I couldn't do *this*.

"Nard, I don't know about this." I mumbled.

He stood up off my bed and proceeded to walk out of the door. Ordinarily for me that would have been my signal to let him walk and never look back, but I wanted him. I didn't just want him sexually, I wanted to be his girl. I don't know why I thought that by having sex with him in such a short amount of time would land me on his arm, but I was about to take a huge gamble in finding out.

"Wait, don't leave, it's cool." I assured him.

"I don't want you doing nothing that you don't want to do. You got me up here feeling like a lil ass teenaged boy." He chuckled.

"No, I'm good. I was just worried about Maliah and Casey coming home." I lied. I knew that they were gone for the night. I just had nothing else to say that would make me sound mature in this situation.

Nard left the lights off, I assumed to keep me comfortable. He began to remove all my clothes. Everything was happening in slow motion. He finally had me stripped down to nothing while he was fully clothed. My knees were weak and my hands were trembling; this was much. I was second guessing everything. *I don't even know him, what am I doing?* The thoughts were quickly dismissed when he kissed me. His hands roamed all over my body and the words he was saying trailed off as I escaped in the unfamiliar feeling of ecstasy. Everything happened fast like it was in the car. It didn't take long before he was naked and laying over top of me ready for action.

My body had never been this aroused *ever*, and I couldn't figure out why I had chosen to wait so long. I even lost decent boyfriends behind my strict no sex policy, but here I was in my bed with practically a stranger about to do it.

Nard tried to enter me but couldn't and all I kept thinking to myself was *relax*.

"How long has it been since you fucked?" He asked bluntly in my ear.

I was so embarrassed by his question that I didn't want to answer him.

"I haven't," I whispered. There was a long pause before he said anything to me.

"This is your first time?" he asked me with disbelief in his voice.

"Yes," I mumbled

Nard sat up on the bed, making me feel dumb as hell. I worried if that was a turn off for him, because he was use to freak ass hoes that had no problem showing him new tricks, and here I was afraid to turn the lights on.

"You should wait it out. I ain't the nigga for this shit." He told me reaching for his shirt.

A sense of disappointment filled my body. My ego had taken a hard hit and I wasn't sure how I was going to recover from it after this. This was *my* decision not his, who was he to tell me who I should wait for? I knew what I was dealing with and I had already decided to take it there with *him*.

"I'm good I can handle myself. I wouldn't have brought you up here if I wasn't sure about it," I was trying to convince him, but not sound too thirsty.

"Lay back down," He instructed and I did exactly what I was told.

Nard placed small kisses all over my waistline. The kisses continued until I felt his lips connect with my clit. The feeling was too much but it was just what I needed to relax.

"You on birth control?" He asked coming up for air.

"Yes," I panted trying to maintain my composure. Maliah made me get a contraceptive the second I started dating, even after I told her I wasn't sexually active.

He abruptly stopped and climbed back on top of me and his soft kisses met my neck as he gently worked to get inside. The pain was overwhelming but with each stroke the feeling became more pleasurable. I could see his handsome face as the moon light beamed on it. I felt like I was in a love making scene in the movies. The feeling of his body on mine alone had to have been the best. The way he smelled, the way he moved and the way he was fucking me was driving me crazy.

"Yesss baby," I moaned in Nard's ear

He sped up and leaned in to kiss me causing his mouth to muffle my moans. We had sex repeatedly that entire night. I knew in my mind *and* heart that he didn't do anything at all to deserve me, but I wanted nothing more than to give him all of me.

~~~~~~~~~

The next morning, I woke up to Nard's sexy face. He was sleeping so peacefully that I didn't want to wake him, but I knew I had to. The last thing I wanted was for Case and Maliah to come home and catch us.

"Wake up," I gently nudging his arm.

He cracked open one eye and reached for his phone that was on my night stand.

"Shit its seven o'clock in the morning." He groaned.

"I know. I don't know what time Case and Maliah will be here."

Nard took his time getting up and going into my bathroom while I sat on my bed in disbelief that I had sex with him last night and loved it. The kids were banging on my room door and yelling that they were hungry. Since Jaylen slept in on the weekend I knew he wasn't going to get up to feed them. He was beating on my door last night, and I was almost sure that he overheard us, so it was only a matter of time before it got back to my sister. He was Maliah's informant; everything he saw and heard was getting back to her.

I waited for Nard to finally come out of the bathroom so that I could follow in after him.

"Damn they're about the break yo' door down." He laughed

"I'm going to distract them, when I come out the bathroom that way you can leave out of here." I told him

"Alright."

In the bathroom while washing up I discovered that almost my entire body was sore to touch which was a sure confirmation that I was not a virgin. I didn't know where we were going to go from this point. It was going to be awkward with me having to see him all the time knowing that we had had sex.

"I'm about to take them downstairs and you can leave without a trace." I smiled.

"Wait, come here before you leave out." He smiled back at me.

I walked over to him and extended my arms for a hug. He held me in his arms for what felt like forever.

"Get some rest after you get them fed. I know you're tired," He told me releasing his hug.

I was beyond tired, and all I wanted to do was sleep. Without a doubt, I was about to sleep the day away. I didn't know what was going to happen next, but I did know I was looking forward to it happening again. Every chance I got I was going to be getting a hit of my new-found addiction. Nard came with every red flag you could think of, but nonetheless I still wanted *him*.

Chapter 8: Maliah

The flight to Chicago was the worst experience for me because Casey was uptight and acting like a nervous wreck. Every five seconds he was blurting out some crazy shit that was making me want to sit in another seat far away from him. I could see why the damn lady didn't want me to bring his ass. He read the Facebook message she sent me a million times.

"She must have been talking about you like a muthafucka for her mama to have found your page," He said

"Yea, tell me about it." I agreed. I was happy that we were coming close to being reunited with Cailey, but I wanted to be left out of this process. I had so much on my heart and brain; I didn't need the extra headache.

When we touched down I couldn't have been happier as I patiently waited in the lobby while Casey made reservations for a rental car. I decided to use the time to check on the kids.

"Hello," Jaylen answered

"Hey Jay, how is everything?" I was a nervous wreck leaving them home while I was out of the state. It was the first time I was this far from them.

"It's cool, Kayla and Aden are in the room watching cartoons."

"Where is Marquita?"

"She's in her room. The door is locked I tried to go in there to check on her." He told me.

That's weird, she never locked her door or ignored my phone calls. I called her over five times. I thought

"Are you sure she's in there?" I questioned

"Yea, she's in there. I thought maybe she was gone but the cars are in the garage and for some reason Nard's car is here but he ain't."

"What? Nard's car is there?!" I didn't know shit about him and I didn't want him snooping around my kids when I wasn't home. I didn't trust him. Any family member of Casey's was not good with me. They hadn't been proven to mean my life any good.

"Jaylen, go to her door and you bang on it until she answers." I instructed.

"Alright"

I heard Jaylen banging on the door like a mad man. I couldn't hear who he was talking to but I assumed it was Marquita.

"She said she has a headache and that she's sleeping." He came back to the phone saying.

"Okay, I'll be home soon. Look after the kids please and call me if you need anything."

Marquita's ass thought that she was slick but I was miles ahead of her. I noticed the way she was staring Nard up and down. I also noticed the way he looked at me letting me know that he wasn't about shit. She had another thing coming if she thought I was going to stand by her fucking with him. I had already made my mind up that we were going back to Michigan. Maybe not Flint, but we were damn sure leaving Boston.

"You ready?" Casey asked with the keys to the rental in his hand.

"Yea, I'm ready."

He drove through the streets of Illinois like a bat out of hell. I held on the door handle to keep from sliding on the leather seats every time he hit the corner doing 60 mph.

"Would you slow the fuck down?!" He was not about to kill me trying to get to where we were going.

When we got to Bridgette's mama's house, her red Mustang was in the drive way. *Oh, my God, please tell me she is not here.* I thought. Before Casey could even put the car in park good enough he was hopping out and on this woman's door banging it down.

"Casey would you stop? This is not *her* house, it's her mother's." I tried to rationalize with him

He didn't hear a word I was saying, he just kept banging until Bridgette finally opened the door. She looked at me like I was scum on the bottom of her shoe. I refused to let her get to me. She had bigger problems than to worry about me; she'd ran off with a crazy nigga's baby. Cailey was on her hip clapping her hands without a care in the world. Casey immediately reached out and retrieved the baby from Bridgette. He stepped inside and sat on a nearby couch just hugging her. It crushed my heart to stand there and witness him finally able to breathe again after seeing his baby girl. No parent should ever have to endure that kind of stress over their child. Bridgette was trash, and she was the perfect example of the baby mama that made a man regret his decision on who he chose to have a baby with.

Mrs. Patterson walked into the living room, and stood in the doorway.

"Hello ma'am, I'm Maliah." I introduced myself

"Hi Maliah." She spoke.

Casey was being rude as hell because he didn't acknowledge the woman standing there, who was clearly terminally ill.

"You called them here?" Bridgette spat at her mother

"Bridgette, you were gone for a week straight with no phone call. I can't take care of my grandbaby. I am sick, and y'all don't give seem to give a fuck!" Mrs. Patterson yelled getting upset.

Bridgette's choice of words got the best of Casey because he stood up off the couch and handed me Cailey.

"Don't give my daughter to her!" Casey snatched up Bridgette by the arm and led her to the door. We had Cailey and now it was time to go back home, there was no need to waste time on Bridgette. I sat Cailey in her play pen and went after him.

"Casey, let's go home! Fuck her, she's not worth it. Cailey is worth it!" I yelled after him

He held Bridgette up against the car and began yelling all type of foul things in her face.

"Casey this is not okay or the place," I said attempting to pull him off her. She was crying hysterically, and blaming me for their break up.

"You gone put me through all of this because of her Case? She turned you against me?!" She screamed. This hoe had lost her mind. I never spoke down on her to him. I was always her problem, but I was going to let her believe whatever her heart desired. If she knew like I knew I would gladly and willingly send his untrustworthy ass right back to her.

Casey finally let her go and he stormed off back into the house. He picked Cailey up from her play pen and placed her into her car seat that was sitting next to the couch on the floor.

"You're not taking her anywhere!" Bridgette yelled coming back into the house

Casey ignored her request and continued to strap Cailey in the car seat.

"Mrs. Patterson, where is her bag?" I asked

She left the room to get the bag while shaking her head back and forth at that chaos that was taking place in her living room. I hate that she had to go through this, and I hated even more that Bridgette was so inconsiderate of her own mother. Cailey and Mrs. Patterson were the only ones keeping me from whooping her ass. To neglect your child and leave her for over a week with your mother that has cancer said a lot about her character. I didn't like her before because of our common interest which was Casey, but now I disliked her because she was a low life.

When Mrs. Patterson came back into the living room with the bag I took it out of her frail hand and I left out to the car. The only person that was losing in this situation was Cailey. She was now about to be separated from her mama after just like she had been separated from her dad.

Casey came out of the house holding the car seat, with Bridgette right behind him. Cailey began to cry from all the commotion. I climbed out and assisted him with putting her in the car. Once she was in I let Casey deal with Bridgette. She wasn't my baby's mama and I didn't have to listen to anything she had to say. She stood in the walkway crying and pleading with him. She wasn't pleading with him not to take Cailey, but pleading that he come back to *her*. I was getting sick just watching this shit. Casey got in the car and she broke down crying in the driveway. Her ass was literally sitting on the pavement in the driveway having a temper tantrum about him leaving her. After hearing her beg him not leave, and noticing that not once did she shed one of those tears for her child, I felt not one ounce of sympathy for her. Bridgette was getting everything that she deserved.

I looked in the backseat at Cailey and smiled at her. She was a beautiful little girl. My mind was going a million miles per hour. I was contemplating my escape from Casey back to Michigan, but now my conscious was bothering me because I didn't want to leave Casey as a single dad. He never turned his back on me when I was struggling with the kids, so a part of me felt in debt to him. I knew I couldn't let this alter my better judgment. The bottom line was I couldn't trust him and I couldn't stay with knowing that's how I felt.

"I apologize about the way I acted," He confessed to me.

"I'm not the one you should be apologizing to. You owe her mama an apology."

I also couldn't wait to get to Boston to get to Marquita. I was upset because I had a feeling she had sex with Nard. I could feel it. His sex appeal was undeniable and I knew the smooth nigga scooped my little sister. I kept calling her phone but she wasn't answering. Even if she answered I wouldn't be able to say much with Casey near me. I was about to shut the entire fuckin operation down as soon as I touched down after this flight.

"What you got on your mind?" He asked me

"I'm just ready to get back and really chill, something I haven't done in a long time," I replied looking at my phone.

"Yea, I want you to take your mind off shit."

I bet you do. I thought

~~~~~~~~~~~~

When I got back to Boston I couldn't get to Marquita's room fast enough. She was sleeping holding her pillow tight. It was three o'clock in the afternoon. I ain't never known her to take a nap, even after studying all day. I walked into her room hand in hand with Aden. I sat him on her bed and told him to wake her up. He went and sat on her head, and started laughing. He lightened the mood, because I was about to let her ass have it.

"Marquita, wake up," I said nudging her arm

"What?" She asked pushing Aden off her neck.

"Get yo' ass up. Why was Nard here last night?" I fumed

"What are you talking about?" She asked with a dumbfounded look on her face.

"Don't play with me, why was he here?" I was trying not to raise my voice, but nothing pissed me off more than a person trying to play with my intelligence.

"We were just chilling." she confessed.

"Marquita I don't have time to play with you, did you fuck him?" I didn't want to hear her answer, but I needed to know. I couldn't believe that I was having this discussion with her. We hadn't been in Boston that damn long. She held her head down and I knew the answer to my question.

"Why Quita? You don't know shit about him." I was furious. I knew what type of nigga Nard was and I did not like the idea of him being intimate with my little sister.

"I like him, Maliah. I don't know why, it's just something about him. He's different from the other guys that I have talked to."

"He's different in a bad way. Nothing positive can come from this. Do you understand that?" I drilled her.

"How do you know what can come from it? I don't get into your personal business so don't get into mine." She defended.

"You know what you're right, but don't come crying to me when he breaks your heart. Just know that y'all ain't about to be meeting up here." I was done saying anything else to her about it. One thing I learned was if a person already has their mind and heart set on doing something then that's what they're going to do.

I gave her a weak smile and left out of her room. I was extremely disappointed in her, but that was not to stop me from preparing myself to pick up the pieces to my sisters soon to be broken heart.

"We got Cailey back, she's downstairs with Case." I informed her

"Where was she?" She asked sitting up in the bed.

"With Bridgette's mama in Chicago."

I have Marquita the details on our adventure to getting Cailey back.

"That girl is crazy, I can't believe she went through all those desperate measurements to keep that man." She shook her head

"You are just as crazy for wanting to mess with someone like Nard. I don't even like how much power you can feel just radiating off him." I shuddered just thinking about how Nard's presence made me feel.

"I think that's what's got me all in to be honest." she admitted

"Yea, you're crazy girl." I told her picking Aden up off the bed to leave the room. "Again, don't say I didn't tell you so." I warned

Chapter 9: Case

I couldn't have been happier to have been reunited with my baby girl. I wanted to snap Bridgette's neck for running off with her. If it wasn't for Maliah stopping me, I can't say that I wouldn't have done just that. It didn't surprise me that she would pull a stunt like that. That was the exact reason I dreaded having a baby by her in the first place. The situation that I was in was getting deep. I had to make a trip back to Michigan to address the shit that was going on in the streets. I could not have niggas out looking for Maliah for any reason.

I drove to Nard's pent house to meet up with regarding our move to Flint. I didn't tell him that I had dipped off to Illinois to get Cailey from Bridgette's simple ass so I figured that he was probably going crazy.

"Yo', where the fuck have you been? Nigga I been calling you. I even stopped by your crib."

"I finally caught up with Bridgette, got Cailey and I brought her back to the crib." I said shaking my head.

"Damn… word?"

"Yeah, but I ain't sweating her. The only common ground that we have now is my baby." He paused. "So, where are we hitting first when we get to Flint?"

"I need to visit ya mama, and see exactly what's going on in these streets," he said.

Nard never referenced my mama as being his, because he had a ton of resent in his heart for her. According to him she didn't give a fuck about him or Lou because both were her step sons, and growing up in the same household together I couldn't say that I disagreed with him. She never wanted her biological kids to be involved in the streets, but she was quick to throw Nard and Lou out to the sharks. Nard was rebellious against Gino as well, but he never talked about why he despised his dad so much. I had reasons to believe it had nothing to do with my mama because even before Gino married her he didn't show love to him.

"We most definitely need to find out exactly what the streets are saying." I agreed.

"So, what you plan on doing with the baby? Maliah cool with her staying with y'all?" He quizzed

Those were questions I didn't have an answer to. Cailey was going to live with me, but I wasn't sure how I was going to pull it off. We had a house full of kids, I felt like I was losing Maliah more and more each day, and I had no idea how our lives were about to play out. What I did know was that I was not about to turn my back on my baby girl.

"Shit, I don't know. I haven't even thought that far ahead. Maliah is going to hold me down nigga. That's the least she can do after how far I've put my shit on the line for her," I said opening his refrigerator.

"Nigga *you* chose to be captain save a hoe, nobody told you to do that shit but you. So, to say that's the least she could do is hoe shit." He shrugged.

I hated to admit it, but he was right. Nard had a harsh way of bringing reality to you, but nonetheless he delivered it real and raw.

"Yea, you're right, but still she better not turn her fuckin back on me," I said grabbing a bottle of water out of the fridge.

"Man, what made this female so special? You ain't even go this hard for Bridgette and she was yo' ride or die." Shook his head trying to make sense of what the question he asked.

"Shit, I ask myself that every day. She cool and her heart is pure. She ain't combative like most of these bitches… she ain't with drama," I replied reminiscing on the history Maliah and I had.

"So, what's good with her lil sis?" He asked with a sneaky smile

"Naw bruh, her head in the books. She don't need to be fuckin around with yo' ass." I laughed.

"Her head is in more than them books, but you ain't even gone give a nigga the benefit of a doubt?"

"Hell no! You ain't never had good intentions with no relationship." I was now laughing hard thinking about Nard's terrible ass relationships back in the day. I could vividly remember him trying to take this female on a date back in the day and she was allergic to the flowers he bought. He snapped on her and threw the flowers in the garbage before he told her that he wasn't taking her nowhere. His patience and ability to manage his emotions were just not there.

"You're right I don't have the instincts to be with no bitch man. They're needy as fuck. I can't do it, don't even want to pretend like I can." He looked off like the thought of settling down was absurd.

He and PJ were two of a kind, only Nard was way rawer and way more cut throat. He would kill a woman if she became too naggy for him, and have no remorse about it afterwards. He was strictly built for war and if you weren't close as kin you had nothing coming.

"Yea, his ass don't need to be in a relationship, he sucks at romance," Aja said walking into the kitchen. She wore nothing but a thong, no shirt, no bra just titties out freely.

"Who told you to come out of the room? And put some fuckin clothes on!" Nard yelled to her.

"Who are you talking to? And last I checked I'm grown, plus you ain't my nigga," She said looking at me with pure seduction in her eyes.

Aja had been working for Nard for years. She never came out to Michigan with him but she stayed on her job back in Massachusetts. She came from a rich ass family so I had no idea why she chose to be in the streets with him. They were never in a committed relationship to my knowledge but they did have some type of sick ass relationship going on. She had been wanting me for a while, but I was never with hitting the same female that my brother was dealing with. In the past I had handed him off a few of them but when it came to vice versa the shit just felt dirty to me, even though Nard didn't give a fuck if I hit any of the females that he dealt with. He didn't have any emotional ties to any of them.

I broke the eye connection we had going on. It only felt right to look in her eyes since she was bold enough to be topless. I had my heart set on being right for Maliah after all that she'd been through. I couldn't slip up with a bitch that belonged to my brother.

"When are you going to let me have some fun with you and that pretty lil thang, Case?" Aja asked me while taking a sip out of a Rose bottle she had gotten out of the refrigerator. She was referencing having a threesome with me and Maliah.

I couldn't help but chuckle at her comment. I could see Maliah slapping the fuck out of me for coming to her with that proposal. "That ain't go happen, Aja," I smiled while visualizing the thought of Maliah's reaction after Aja gave her head. I know she loved it even though she wouldn't admit it to me.

"You sure about that?" she smirked

"Man take yo' thirsty ass up outta here." Nard told her causing me to laugh harder. "These bitches are worse than niggas," he shook his head at her forwardness.

"You sound like you jealous, Nard," Aja challenged him

I couldn't understand why she always said the shit that she did to him. He was the same nigga I had to grow up constantly telling that hitting females wasn't cool. He went from that to killing if it meant a payday for him, but Aja loved pressing his buttons. It was almost as if the shit turned her on.

"Man, get the fuck out of my face." he countered.

She began to laugh like he was the funniest man on earth.

"NOW!!" Nard roared

Aja scurried off to the bedroom, titties bouncing and all.

"Sick ass bitch." he mumbled.

The rest of the day I spent with Nard chopping up our plan on returning to Michigan. We had so much to execute on. Our pops were meeting us there too and it would be the first time that I touch bases with him since all this shit happened.

Chapter 10: Marquita

Today was my eighteenth birthday and it also marked exactly two weeks since I had sex with Nard. He stopped coming in our house when he was over to see Case which led me to believe that he was avoiding me. We didn't exchange numbers that night so it wasn't like I could call him. I told myself that I would be understanding to the fact that he wanted me to treat it like it was nothing more, and nothing less than sex but that was getting harder by the day for me. I lied and told him I could handle it being just sex, but Nard knew that I had given him my virginity, so I was sure that he was a lot smarter than that to believe that I could handle no strings attached. I overheard Case tell Maliah that they were going back to Flint tomorrow so I was hoping, praying and wishing that he would pull up on me at least once before he left.

I was self-consciously taking more time on my hair and makeup, as well as coordinating outfits together longer than usual just in case he popped up. No nigga had ever had a hold on me like this. I would often fantasize about the night I had with him. I was still having trouble believing it. I sat on my bed texting my home girl from school back in Detroit and playing toy cars with Aden. Life was so damn boring, so I stayed on Maliah's head to take us back home. She was losing her mind trying to get Cailey to warm up to her and chase behind Aden. He was jealous they had brought another baby in here and had been acting a damn fool about it.

"This is how you celebrate your birthday? Playing with cars?" My heart stopped hearing Nard's voice as I looked over to the door at him.

"It's nothing else to do in this boring state, and it's not like you've been coming around." I responded giving my attention back to Aden.

"Chill the fuck out. I've been busy so I haven't had time to come through. Won't you come take a ride with me." he suggested.

"Naw, I'm good. I rather spend my day playing cars with my nephew." I knew damn well that I wanted to be out and about with him but I had to play it cool. I couldn't let him know that I was pressed. If I let him know how thirsty I was then he would treat me like a door mat and show up whenever he felt like it.

"Man, come on I don't have time for you to being playing this role. You know you want to roll. What you tryin' to stand yo' ground? You mad I ain't been coming in to say hi to you?" he smiled.

Nard was reading the shit out of my mind. Aden began launching cars across the room because I stopped playing with him. The little boy had a bad temper that his parents chose to do nothing about.

"You see? He's angry that I stopped playing with him." I laughed.

"Alright continue your play date, I'll holla at you some other time," He said texting on his phone.

He was unbelievable, his level of no fucks was far from what I was used to. I wanted him to stand there and keep asking me to leave with him like most of the needy niggas that I had dealt with in the past, but clearly that was not going to happen. Nard was nothing like *those* niggas.

Letting out a long sigh, because I was sad that this was what my birthday had come to. I had to have had the lamest life ever. I wasn't going to sit at home bored on my birthday, so I decided to leave Aden with his mama to let her spend all day entertaining him. Maliah bought me a cake and some gifts but that didn't make me feel like turning eighteen was something special. I grabbed the car keys off the counter and made my way to Maliah's ELR I was going to get out today and see what this boring city had to offer my bored ass. I arrived at Cambridge Mall, and the parking lot was jammed pack. After circling the lot twice, I found a parking space. I put on my oversized Chanel sunglasses and made my way to the entrance. I felt down that I didn't have anyone to call to shop with but I was going to make the best of the trip. I figured since I was there I could find me an outfit to wear for my birthday dinner with the family later.

I strolled through the mall impressed by the selections that it had to offer. Case had given me more than enough money for my birthday to buy myself something nice. He had been working overtime to keep us all satisfied. Everyone in the house could sense the tension between him and Maliah and although she hadn't told me all their personal problems, I knew that it was serious enough to draw a huge wedge between the two of them. Kayla, Jaylen and I weren't complaining though, because Case was barely saying no to anything these days.

"Hey, excuse me, do you have a minute?"

I broke the attention that I had on the Alexander Wang dress and focused on the voice that belonged to a handsome young guy. His caramel skin was blemish free and glowing. The thick black curls in his low hair cut naturally shined under the mall lighting and his defined jawline was perfect for the half smile he gave me. He was for sure a cutie but I wasn't sure why he had approached me.

"Yes?" I asked

"My brother wanted to come talk to you but he's shy as hell," He said with a straight face.

I could not control my laugh as I burst out into an uncontrollable laugh. It was funny to me because The Five Heartbeats was my favorite movie and all I could think of was Duck and J.T with their shy brother game. I peeked over his shoulder and spotted a tall dark guy that wasn't nearly as cute as Mr. handsome here in my face. The guy was unattractive to me, and the only nice looking about him were his clothes. He was fly but definitely not *my* type. He looked familiar, but I couldn't put my finger on where I knew him from.

"Does this really work for y'all?" I asked no longer laughing because I seriously needed answers.

He gave me a confused look like he has no idea what I was talking about.

"Does what work?"

"Okay, I'm done here. Tell your brother that he should have enough balls to approach a woman himself. Like seriously how old are y'all?"

I redirected my attention back to the dress and dismissed him still standing there. If this was what Massachusetts had to offer, then I was a lot further than what I thought to gaining a social life.

The rest of my shopping trip I thought about Nard. I was wishing that I wasn't so stubborn at times. I had my sights set on him and only him, but it was going to be hard for me to follow up with a nigga after him. Crazy thing was he was never even mine and I was already hooked. I walked out the door to the car with shopping bags galore. I had picked up the kids a few things too. Not that they needed anything, but I stayed being a sucker when it came to them.

As I got closer to the car I noticed the two wack ass kids that were in the mall parked directly next to me. Mr. unattractive was the driver and the car he was leaning up against had my mouth hanging to the floor. Everything about them screamed rich Boston kids, but the McLaren P1 that he was driving said that we weren't just talking a little rich. Driving a 1.1-million-dollar car was a whole lot of rich. He was still ugly and childish so I wasn't changing my mind on my impression of him. I politely walked past his car to get to Maliah's car.

"So, you ain't gone let me talk to you?" He asked

"*You* didn't ask to talk to me, you sent another man to speak for you." I snapped

Mr. Unattractive stood up from leaning on the car and walked over to me. *I don't have time for this shit.*

"I apologize about that. My bro thinks doing that shit is funny. I didn't send him over to talk to you." He smiled

His Boston accent was cute, so was his smile, but he was not.

"My name is Dontae," he introduced himself and extended his hand.

"I'm Marquita, nice to meet you," I said accepting his hand shake.

"So, what are you doing tomorrow Marquita?" He asked never taking his eyes off mine.

I didn't have a life. The only plans I had was playing a couple of Uno card games with Kayla. That had become my weekend ritual. I refused to share those plans with him so I responded with, "Nothing".

"I'm having a pool party at my house tomorrow night if you want to fall through. If you give me your number I can text you my address," He said pulling his phone out of his pocket

I gave off my number to him and left the mall. I debated on going to his party the entire drive back to my house. I didn't know anyone and I didn't want to look stupid standing alone. I had just dismissed the idea of going to the party when my phone vibrated. It was a text message from Dontae.

3476 Bay ridge Circle. Boston, MA. I hope to see you there beautiful

I closed the text message and pulled into our community gates. Nard was parked in front of our walk way. My heart began to pound fast in my chest as he opened the driver's door and got out. I couldn't keep this up. I was going to have a fuckin heart attack if I did. I didn't look him over when I saw him earlier that day but I had a full view now and he was sexy as ever. I was hoping that he would attend my birthday dinner that was tonight. He had on a wife beater and was dripping in diamonds. I was arguing with myself in my head for me to play it cool. *Why in the fuck am I so nervous?* I parked the car and got out. He walked passed me without saying a word and went into the house. I wanted to cry right there on the spot. *That's what I get for fuckin him in the first place.* I kicked myself mentally. I left my bags in the car to hurt to care about them. I slammed the car door and stormed into the house. Nard was nowhere in sight but Maliah was right at the door as soon as I walked in.

"What is wrong with you?" She asked in shock

"I'm fine!" I was clearly not fine and her facial expression told me that she was not buying it.

"You're not fine, Marquita. I'm going to tell you something and this will be the last time I tell you. He is not what you need at all unless you like feeling how you do now. Leave it alone, and I'm not going to tell you again. We will be moving soon because I can see already this is not going to work out." She warned again.

I heard everything my sister was telling me, but I could not for the life of me figure out why my heart wanted Nard to be its owner. I was downright infatuated with him. When I was back home I would call girls stupid for fuckin with guys like him and here I was now one of those girls. He had made me his fool quick. I didn't like the burning sensation in my heart from when I would get my hopes up thinking he would come by to see me.

Maliah went into the kitchen to feed Cailey, Kayla and Aden lunch. I went the opposite direction to get myself together in the bathroom. *This is not okay,* I heard Maliah's words in my head and I hated the way my heart burned in my chest. Nard had walked passed me as if I didn't exist. I could see now the harder I played hard to get the more he would be unfazed. That wasn't going to work with him. In my mind if I wanted him I had to be submissive otherwise I didn't have anything coming. I reached the bathroom and out came Nard.

He scared me half to death as I jumped. I refused to say anything to him, because I wasn't going to let him know that I was hurting.

As I walked passed him he grabbed my arm to my surprise.

"Come here," he said pulling my arm to the bathroom with him. He closes the door behind him.

"What are you doing? Maliah is right in the kitchen." I was terrified my sister would catch me, but I was also happy to be back in his presence, so it felt worth the risk.

"Why haven't I seen you until now?" I whispered but he didn't answer me. My question hung in the air as he kissed me with so much passion. My body immediately responded to his. He stuck his hand down in my shorts and began to play with my clit.

In the mist of his ecstasy I removed his hand from my shorts. I didn't want to become his play object but it appeared it was too late for me not to be.

"This shit is wrong," I said to him in between moans

Nard didn't stop to honor my request and I didn't push for him to stop. I wanted him to keep going, I was giving him my heart to break into a billion pieces. All that would come from this would be a raft of hurt, but this was the one wave I was more than willing to ride. The bathroom spun around my head in circles until I had a massive orgasm. Before I could come down from the high Nard had my shorts off and was inside of me. I held onto the sink and allowed us both to get caught up in the moment. I forgot that my entire family was just feet away in the house. Today was my first day as an adult and I was already making my first bad decision, and that was falling hard for the wrong guy; a guy that would never love me.

Nard continued to penetrate me until his body locked and he released inside of me.

"Shit." he groaned while helping me off the sink.

I turned the faucet on and remained silent. I felt like a puppet and Nard was in full control of the strings.

"I don't have your number to even hit you up," I said finally breaking the silence

"Yea, I thought about that afterwards. Where is your phone?" he responded.

I had thrown my small cross purse on the floor when he pulled me into the bathroom. I bent down and rumbled through it until I could grab my phone out.

"617-567-9867, text me so I'll know it's you." He told me.

I was doing cart wheels on the inside. I had a glimmer of hope that it may be a possibility that I could make him my man exclusively. I washed up and hurried out of the bathroom before I got caught. I would take a long hot bath while thinking about Nard in my own personal bathroom.

"You want to spend the rest of your birthday with me?" he asked.

I didn't waste any time thinking about it because I didn't want him to renege on his offer. I knew that he wasn't going to ask me twice.

"Yea, let me just take a quick shower and grab my things." I said with no hesitation.

I dreaded explaining to Maliah that I was canceling my birthday dinner with them tonight, but she would have to understand that this was *my* life and *my* birthday.

Nard kissed my forehead before we parted ways causing my heart to thump in my chest. He went to wait in the car for me.

The rest of the evening consisted of us getting a carry out and me being turned out by him in his bachelor pad. Until I could officially make him mine he would be mine in my mind and unfortunately this is what I would be settling for.

Chapter 11: Maliah

I was catching hell with all these fuckin kids and I was becoming more and more resentful of Casey. He had me living out in the middle of nowhere, I was taking care of 4 kids, and worried about Marquita's now grown ass. She thought I was stupid but I knew her hot ass was still snooping behind Nard. I had no problem with caring for Cailey, because I loved her for simply belonging to Casey, but caring for her and all the other kids was taking it's toll on me.

Ms. James was a big help but I couldn't bring myself to be comfortable with another woman caring for them. In my mind, I felt like no one could care for the kids like I could.

"Hey Baby, what you in here doing?" Casey asked

"I'm on Facebook reading Bridgette's inbox threats of her killing herself if we don't bring Cailey back."

She had been in-boxing me nonstop. I was not an advocate of a parent keeping a child from the other parent. Casey was doing the exact same thing that she done to him.

"Man, fuck her, you need to block her."

"Maybe you should hear her out and set up a visitation schedule with her. Both of y'all need to grow up." I huffed while laying Cailey down in her bed. She had fallen asleep on my lap.

"Alright, I see it's stressing you so I'll reach out to her in the morning. I don't know why you care. She doesn't give a fuck about you, and you know it," He said sounding obligated

"Casey, what really happened the night Eriq was murdered? And keep it real with me."

I was still having nightmares every night and I needed answers and closure. He sat on the bed like I had just asked him the most irritating question on earth.

"I told you I didn't know, yet you keep asking me this shit. I didn't have the hit placed on him. The nigga was in the streets so it's no telling where it came from." He told me.

"I don't believe or trust you, and because I don't believe or trust you I can't be with you. I'm only here because I don't want my family in danger." I confessed

"You have no reason not to trust me. All my wrongs are out there and you telling me that you can't be with me for some shit that I didn't do? That's fucked up!"

"No what's fucked up is the fact that my baby daddy got killed right in front of me, and I lost my mama in the same token. Your family had something to do with this shit and I'm not stopping until I find out who. When I do, you better believe it will be consequences." I threatened

I was sick of Casey's shit. I had Shawnie working overtime back home getting me information off the street, because he had another thing coming if he thought I was staying in Boston with him with my head in the clouds.

"Go head and investigate some shit. We can solve the fuckin mystery together." He said in a sarcastic tone

Casey was leaving that night to head back to Flint and I was going to use that time to connect with some people back home on getting more information on what went down that night. He made it hard for me to talk to anyone living out of town. So, I was going to take full advantage of the opportunity.

"Do you know anything about Nard and Marquita? I don't trust him and I don't want him coming around here. You can go visit him at his house." I was jumping from subject to subject because I had so many things bothering me.

"Know something like what? And what did he do to make you not trust him?" He asked with concern.

"I don't like the idea that he has been coming over here and messing around with Marquita. He isn't right and my instincts never lie, his vibes are off."

"Alright, he'll stop coming by here. I don't want you to feel uncomfortable, but you should know we can't control what they do, it's not your business." I rolled my eyes at his comment. I was past being uncomfortable. I was ready to go back home before the plane even landed in this state, and Casey was wrong, my sister was *my* business.

My notifications indicated that I had a new message on my phone. It was from Shawnie.

I ran into April at the mall and her ass took off running when she saw me.

Shawnie's message read. I could believe it because April was all mouth unless she felt like someone protected her else. Ayesha was in hiding, I had staked out at her house for weeks and she never popped up. Flint wasn't big so her ass had to have skipped town because she knew what she was facing if I ever laid eyes on her again. Casey kept telling me not to worry because he would have it handled but I wanted revenge on my own. Ayesha had crossed me in the worst way. I wanted April's ass too but it was on different level than Ayesha. She betrayed me and pretended to be my friend but despised me the entire time that I was around her. It was so crazy to me that you had to get out of the presence of someone to think back and observe that they never had good intentions for you from the beginning. The bitch showed had every red flag there was that she didn't want me to be great.

"And why do you think him and Marquita have been fuckin around?" Casey's eyebrows furrowed together as he awaited my answer.

"I have my reasons, Casey.I It's just crazy how oblivious you can be to certain situations." I explained

He pondered what I said to him.

"I'll get to the bottom of it," He said packing his suitcase. I eyed his muscular arms and chest in his Versace t-shirt. He had just gotten a fresh haircut and his waves were swimming deep. I hadn't been emotionally connected with him to notice how handsome he still was.

"Casey next month I'm going back to Michigan. I understand you wanting to protect us, but I have somethings that I have to sort out. We aren't even together for you to have me on the run with you."

"You not going back to Michigan, Maliah. If you don't want to live with me I'll get another spot, but after all you went through back there I can't let you go back." That vein began to bulge again that let me know he meant business. I was done telling him what I had planned on doing, I was just going to do.

A Knock on the door disturbed our conversation that was leading to being heated.

"Come in," Casey ordered

Ms. James walked into the bedroom.

"Nard and Aja are down stairs waiting on you Casey." She informed.

"Thank you." he nodded she left back out of the bedroom

"Alright baby, I'm about to go. I'll see you in two weeks. If you need anything call me, but I know you're going to hold it down." He reached out to hug me. He wrapped me in his strong arms and held me tight. It felt good to be in his embrace, and as much as I hated to admit to myself two weeks without him was going to be hard for me. The love I had for him was immeasurable. It was just so fucked up that our relationship had been sabotaged the way it had been.

"Just be safe, Casey. I'm not emotionally right to take anymore hurt." I sighed

"I'm always good, you know that," He said looking in my eyes. I grabbed on the handle of his roller bag and helped him take it out to the car so that he could depart.

Upon entering the living room Nard was sitting on the couch next to Aja. I didn't like either one of their asses and with each passing day they both rubbed me wrong. Aja smiled at me licking her lips. I turned my head from her and spoke dryly to Nard.

"Hi," I threw my hand up and waved

"Hi Maliah. It's good seeing you." He responded.

"We don't have much time our plane leaves soon," Nard looked at his watch anxious by what it read.

He and Casey took his luggage out to the car leaving Aja and me alone.

"So, how long have you and Case been together?" She asked.

"We aren't together." I responded.

"Oh? It seems like you are. He looks so happy when he's with you."

"Everything ain't always what it seems." I snapped.

I didn't want to make small talk with her. I had no desire to be friendly with her. She gave me the vibe that she was the type to fuck your man and give zero fucks about it; especially after the way she violated me with Casey laying right next to me. I wasn't about to play with her, because I would definitely fuck her up. Just as I was walking away Aden came running full speed into the room with Kayla in his tracks.

He was holding her Barbie by the hair laughing.

"Sissy, he is ruining her hair, and I just did it." she whined

The older Aden got the more he drove her crazy. He stayed into Salk of her things and she wanted nothing more than for him to stay away.

"Aden! Give Kayla back her doll." I scolded him. With a guilty look on his face he did as I ordered.

Kayla looked down at the doll he handed over to her with disgust. The dolls hair was messy and standing straight up.

"He destroys everything." She cried storming out the room

"He's a little terror I see." Aja laughed

I didn't respond to her. I held Aden's hand until Casey came back into the house. Marquita walked into the living room while I impatiently waited. Her shorts were tiny and the half shirt displayed her perfect abs that she got from going so hard for in the gym. Her mood immediately switched when she seen Aja sitting on the couch.

"What's going on in here?" She asked

"Nothing, I'm waiting on Casey to come back in so we can tell him bye," I responded.

"Oh, they're leaving today?" Marquita asked like she should have been informed they were leaving.

"Yea, they're leaving today. What Nard ain't tell you?" Aja smirked

We both looked at her like she was out of line. Marquita had a very short temper and it didn't take much for her to beat some ass. This was the exact reason I don't want her dealing with Nard. He screamed drama and nothing about him spoke positive; not even his *assistant*.

"What the fuck did you just say?" Marquita asked with venom in her voice

"I'm sorry, did I say something wrong? I figured Nard would have told you since you have a little crush on him." Aja smiled

"Bitch, you're fuckin with the wrong one." Marquita charged at Aja like a bat out of hell. I grabbed her arm and used all my force to pull her back. She was not about to fight, especially while Aden was standing there.

"Marquita, fuck her. She won't be back here." I assured her.

"I teach bitches lessons who like to open their mouths when I ain't ask them to." Marquita threatened.

Just as it was getting harder for me to restrain my sister, Case and Nard walked back in. Nard immediately went for Marquita and held her arms to her side.

"What's going on?" He asked her.

"Fuck you and fuck her!" Marquita snapped with tears falling from her eyes.

Aja said nothing. Instead she stood up and brushed past Casey headed out the door.

"What the fuck did we just miss? You can't leave females together for a minute without it being some bullshit." Casey laughed

"This shit ain't funny, I want you to stay the fuck from around here, and around her." I pointed at my sister. "Nobody has time to deal with this." I warned Nard

"Get your fuckin hands off me!" Marquita snatched away from Nard's grip.

"Yo', bring your ass outside," he said to Marquita.

"She's not going anywhere with you." I intervened

Casey had taken Aden out of the living room into the back with Kayla and Cailey. Without acknowledging me at all Nard stared Marquita down. She shied away from his eye contact.

"Now, because that wasn't a question." He demanded

Like a sick puppy Marquita walked over to the door and onto the porch leaving me blown away. This was not my sister; she was not weak when it came to anything and damn sure not over a nigga. I stood there shaking my head when Casey approached me.

"Baby, I won't bring them back over here. Whatever it takes to keep the peace I'm doing it." Casey tried reassuring me, but I was more concerned with my sister being outside with Nard.

"I don't know who the fuck he thinks he is, but I also don't want him around her," I was furious at the way he talked to her.

"I'm going to talk to the both, but you have to keep in mind that's all I can do. You remember what it was like to be eighteen, no one could tell you anything."

"Eighteen? That's not grown," I said in defense.

"Maliah she just turned eighteen this week, so stop it. Like I said, I'll talk to them." Casey kissed my forehead and said his goodbyes to the kids.

I sat on the couch waiting for Marquita to come back in the house. She knew she would have to face me and that's why she sat on the stairs before coming in. She knew better than that. I had no problem with going out to meet her and get what I had to say off my chest.

"Would you like to talk to me about something?" I asked taking a seat next to her.

"Nope, I don't." she was looking at her phone screen and not giving me her undivided attention like I wanted.

"I feel like you need to tell me something. Aja, asking you a question about him sent you in a frenzy."

"I just told you I'm straight. I don't want to talk about the shit," She said to me with an attitude.

"Okay, I'm out of it. I forgot you're grown now." I countered sarcastically.

"I'm out of here, I need to clear my head," She said standing up to go into the house to get the car keys.

If I didn't know anything else, I knew that you couldn't tell someone something that knew it all already. In the meantime, I was executing my plan the fuck away from here.

Chapter 12: Marquita

I couldn't believe that bitch tried to play me out like that. It was obvious Nard had been telling her our business. Although I was pissed at her and him, I was even madder with myself. I signed up for this shit the second that I opened my legs for him. I just didn't think that my intuition would be right. I was hoping that it proved me wrong. Aja was more than his assistant otherwise she wouldn't have been talking to me like she had just done, or show up to my house looking for him. To make matters worse Nard came pulling me outside telling me that I was the one in my feelings. He was just in the bathroom fuckin me but turned on me quick when drama was presented, and had the nerve to say that I was the one in my feelings and I needed to chill out. I had taken more than enough for one day so I decided to take Dontae up on his offer to go to his pool party.

I retrieved his address from my phone and jumped on the highway in the direction to his house. I desperately needed something to take my mind off the shit that had just happened. When I got to the house I second guessed the location because the house I was supposed to be coming too was not where my GPS informed me that I had arrived. It was nothing but an open road and a gate. I assumed that behind the gates led to his house. I called him to make sure he sent me the correct information.

"Hello." He answered in his thick Boston accent

"Hey, Dontae. It's Marquita. Where exactly do you live... I think I'm here?"

"Are you in front of black steel gates?" He asked

"Yes." I replied

As soon as I responded the gates slowly opened. The shit was creepy as hell, it had me second guessing my decision to come here.

"Follow the path, it leads to my house. I'll meet you in the front."

I followed his instructions and drove down the path. I shot Maliah his address via text, just in case something happened to me I wanted her to know where to come looking. The path was damn near a mile long. When it finally ended, I had to rub my eyes and do a double take. I was driving toward a beautiful house, this house made ours look like we were back living in the projects in Flint. The mansion had to have been over eight thousand square feet. Outside of the house were sculpted shrubs and the cars that sat out front were valued together more than three million dollars. *Who in the fuck is this kid related to?*

As he stated Dontae was standing in front of the house in a pair of Gucci swim trunks with matching flip flops on his feet. He looked slightly better than when I saw him at the mall. He walked over to the car and opened the door.

"I'm happy you could make it," He said smiling.

"Thanks for inviting me." I was embarrassed that I didn't come in swimming attire. I was so mad at the Nard situation I didn't grab anything to wear to the party.

We walked side by side through the humongous house. He had a butler, a nanny; hell, the nigga even had rich ass dogs. The two Tibetan Mastiff's collars had to have been more expensive than anything I owned.

"Your house is beautiful." I spoke up

"It's not my house, it's my dad's house, but thank you. Are you thirsty, or hungry?"

"No, I'm fine. Thank you." I couldn't stop staring at all of the antique furniture that was throughout the house. It looked like it all cost a fortune.

"Is that who live with? Your dad?" I asked

"Yea, but he's not here often. I'm almost always here on some solo shit. My sister comes over every occasionally." He said opening a sliding door that lead to an indoor/outdoor Olympic size pool. I noticed that the ceiling retracted and currently making it an outdoor pool for the party. It was filled with people, some in the pool, and some lounging around the outdoor bar. It looked like a scene off Project X. These were a bunch of rich teenaged kids that wouldn't survive a day where I was from.

I walked around the party with Dontae as he introduced me to some of his friends.

"Come on we can sit over there and get to know one another." he smiled.
I had to admit his personality was very charming. I examined his smiling face to see if I could point out exactly what it was about him that I found unattractive. He had no obvious ugly features, but I couldn't pinpoint what was off the way he looked to me.

We sat off to the side in a nearby sunroom.

"So where are you from? I can hear from the way you talk that you're a long way from home." He laughed

"I'm from Michigan, you're right that is a long way from here. And I can tell by the way you talk that you are right at home." I replied

"I'm from Manchester, that's where I was born and raised. My mom was from there, and my dad is from N.Y. She passed away when I was a baby and my dad just decided to raise us in her home state." He said

"I'm sorry about your loss, I recently lost my mama too." I sighed thinking about Rosie. When she was alive I didn't think that I would care one way or the other if she was dead, but now that she was gone I couldn't talk about her without tearing up.

"Damn, sorry to hear that, who do you live with here?" He asked

I liked how smoothly the conversation was flowing with Dontae. It was easy talking to him. I wasn't nervous, he was attentive, and his responses were on point. The niggas I talked to these days always had some crazy shit flying out of their mouth, or everything was about sex. Talking to him was therapeutic and we were only a few questions in. The party was live, and although the sunroom was sound proof I could see that everyone was thoroughly enjoying themselves.

"I live with my older sister, her ex-boyfriend, my brother, baby sister, my niece and nephew." I said overly dramatic. I was awaiting his response to it, but to my surprise he nodded his head.

"That's cool, a house full sounds good to me. I'm always up in here lonely as hell. Maybe you can come over to keep me company." He suggested

I would move the fuck in this nice ass house if I could.

"That sounds like a good idea to me." I said smiling from ear to ear.

"So you got a man Marquita?" I knew this question was coming and I didn't know how to answer. I didn't have a man per say, but I did have sex with someone that I was infatuated with hours before I got to his house.

"No, I'm single. How about you?" I dismissed all thoughts of Nard with hopes of starting something new with Dontae.

"No, I think I want you as bae." He smiled at me

"Me as bae? That's a nice gesture. How old are you?" I knew we weren't too far apart in age but I also knew that we were cut from a different cloth. I had lived a life that had been filled with struggles and he had come from a privileged life.

"I'm seventeen, this is my senior year, you?"

"Yesterday was my birthday, and I'm finishing up my first semester of college" I informed him.

"Yesterday was your birthday? Damn you're spending your eighteenth birthday weekend here with me?" he asked surprised.

"I am." I laughed at how he was in disbelief.

"We really gotta get this party turned up." He said standing up.

"No, this is cool. I'm liking conversing with you. Let's keep it at this level. Pretend like I didn't just tell you yesterday was my birthday." I pleaded for him not to make my birthday a big deal.

This was the most comfort I had experienced since moving to Boston and I didn't want to end it so quickly.

"Alright, I'll try to ignore that you just told me that...you graduated high school early? He questioned

"Yea, I skipped a grade or two." I shrugged laughing

We sat talking for hours, it wasn't long before the party was *really* like a scene from Project X. All the minors there were drunk and high and Dontae made sure the shit was kept outside he was on high alert when someone tried to go in his house. The damn butler was outside partying too. He needed his ass kicked for partying this hard with these kids. I was happy that I decided to come over; this was the most fun I'd had in a long time.
Nard was texting me, and as bad as I wanted to ignore his texts I couldn't stop replying to them in between conversations with Dontae.

Nard: *I apologize about what went down earlier, she doesn't usually interfere with my personal life this much*

Me: *No need to apologize I pictured shit going this way*

Nard: *If I ever apologize to you then there is a need for it, so stop trippin'...now*

I loved and hated his cocky ass demeanor at the same. He had to be in control of every situation and it got on my nerves often, but there were other times when I would smile because I thought it was his way of showing that he cared. I slid my phone into my pocket, and enjoyed the rest of my stay at Dontae's house.

~~~~~~~~~~~~~~~

When I got home that night all the kids were sleeping in Jaylen's room with the door closed. I followed the sounds of Maliah's cries coming out of her bedroom.

"What's wrong sis?" I asked taking a seat next to her on the floor.

Before she could answer Jaylen walked into the room with us. "She's been crying like this for hours and not saying anything. I put the kids to sleep and left her to get it all out." He brought me up to speed with what was going on with Maliah.

I felt low about how I treated her earlier when she was only concerned about my well-being. I hadn't taken into consideration all that she had been through and was still going through. I embraced her in my open arms and she had a meltdown.

"Okay, I have it from here Jay, you can get some sleep." I comforted my brother

"I'm tired Marquita, I can't take anymore. I want to go home. I can't stay here and pretend nothing happened. And I found this letter in Casey's shit" she cried handing me a folded piece of paper. I opened it to read over it and it was a letter from a bitch in jail saying how she couldn't wait to be released so that they could be together. It was signed by someone by the name of Brandy, but when I looked at the date it was from two years ago.

"I know, we can go back. I'm down to go home too, and that letter is old as fuck though. I wouldn't give that any thought sis" I said in agreement but wanting her not to stress irrelevant shit and that letter was *highly* irrelevant.

"No, you're staying here with the kids. I need to go for a few days and when I come back, I'll be coming to get y'all." She sternly said to me

"Okay, whatever you want to do just let me know." I hugged her whishing that it was some way I could take away the pain that she was feeling.

It broke my heart to see her in this state. I ran her bath water, laid her pajamas out on her bed and poured her a glass of wine from the bar Case had set up.

"Get some rest Maliah" I closed her bedroom door with hopes that she would take my advice.

Chapter 13: Case

The long ass drive to Michigan from Massachusetts drained the life from me. We couldn't fly back home because I didn't need flights being traced back to me. I needed to be able to slip in and out.

"Nigga pull over at the next gas station." I instructed to Nard.

"Fuck no, we almost there. I'm tired of driving." He complained

"*Almost there?* We are in fuckin Monroe, nigga that's over an hour until we get to Flint!" I yelled. He had me fucked up not wanting to pull the car over.

"Damn, you about to set me back with this stop, you ain't know you had to piss at the last stop?" he questioned me

I pointed to the exit coming up, I wasn't about to argue with him about me needing to stop. Either way it went we had to keep driving until we got to where the fuck we were going.

The next exit he got off and stopped us at a McDonalds. I wasted no time getting out to take a piss. His impatient ass wasn't trying to stop for shit. I walked in and darted straight to the restroom.

After talking all of that shit about stopping Nard decided to come inside too. The twelve-hour car ride had the nigga straight tripping to the point I wasn't ever riding in a car with him again.

While we were walking out of the restroom I looked in the eyes of a woman exiting the women's restroom at same time we were. She was an employee at McDonald's and from the look on her face you would have thought she was looking at Michael Meyers. My eyes looked up at the ceilings to see if there were any cameras around. The only cameras in the restaurant were facing the cash registers. I pulled my gun out and kept it close to my side and I nodded my head toward the door for her to go back into the restroom. Nard stood on the outside of the door guarding it as I forced her back inside. I was hoping no one else would be in there, and it was my lucky day because it was empty.

Nard was a professional in the line of killing so I knew that it was bothering him standing on the outside of the door while I was preparing to get my hands dirty alone. I had to handle this particular situation myself.

"Ca Case, you don'tt understand." Ayesha stuttered.

"It ain't shit to understand." I stated with ice dripping from my words.

"Your mama gave two g's to April and me to beat up Maliah. I felt so horrible afterwards." She began to cry.

I was fucked up from what she had just told me. *My mama paid them?* I thought to myself.

"She told us that if we didn't do it that she would hire someone else to do it and someone beat our asses." She explained.

I couldn't hear anymore words that were coming out of her mouth because I was sick to my stomach by the news she just dropped on me.

Outraged I grabbed her neck and began to strangle the life out of her. Her hands clawed at my arms but no scratches were left because of the thick hoodie that I had on. I hated a snake and Ayesha was a snake from day one. Before they jumped Maliah, she was hating telling me everything there was to know with hopes that I would leave her. If my mama did ask them to hurt her I knew that Ayesha didn't have an ounce of regret afterwards. Her only regret was coming to work today. Her lifeless body was propped on the toilet as I smooth and quickly made it back out into the car.

Nard pulled out of the parking lot talking shit about how long I had taken in there. It blew my mind how he didn't have a stitch of paranoia in him during the remainder of the drive to Flint. I couldn't say the same for myself killing was not second nature for me. It was fucked up that it had to go down that way. Those bitches left Maliah for dead and I could sleep better knowing that I was able to partially take care of the situation. Nard continued to cruise down the freeway as if it never happened.

The fact that she told me my mama had something to do with it set me on fire. Every bad thing in Maliah's life was being traced back to my fuckin family. I had no idea why in the fuck would my mama want them to hurt her the way that they had, but I was about to find out. I had enough of the fuck shit that everyone was on. If I was happy it shouldn't have mattered if she had 100 kids living in a box, but that wasn't the case. My mama was livid that I loved Maliah but what I didn't know was that she would go so low, and to foul ass measurements to see us not together.

After Ayesha pulled a disappearing act I wasn't taking a chance of her doing it again and justice never being served. Who knew that she started a new life in Monroe and worked at McDonalds. She and April almost killed Maliah the night they attacked her, I couldn't let her get away with it after she posed as a so-called friend to her for so many years. Nard was very familiar with what Ayesha had done. When I told him about it he couldn't believe it. We all grew up hanging out in the hood and seeing Ayesha was always seeing Maliah. Shit was crazy how your enemies can be closer than what you think.

I was in deep thought the remainder of the ride and I didn't notice that we were coming up on the exit to Flint. It felt weird being back in the city after being gone a minute. Our first stop was a house my mama owned that we would be staying it. It was low key, and no one would find us there. Nard and I immediately disposed of the clothes we wore because we didn't want any evidence from me killing Ayesha on us.

Once I was out of the shower and settled in the bedroom I would sleeping in for the next week I was greeted by my mama coming in the front door.

"Boy, have you lost your damn mind?!" Was the first thing she asked me

"Man fuck you, you had those hoes fight Maliah!!?!" I snapped without thinking twice. I didn't care about the fact that she was my mama. If she was a real mother to me I wouldn't be going through half the shit that I was going through. She was the reason behind me being stressed out.

"Yea you have lost yo' damn mind, that girl has you all up in her tea." She said while shaking her head.

Up in her tea? What the fuck does that mean? I thought with my face screwed up.

"You ain't about to talk your way out of this shit, did you or did you not pay them to attack her?!" I asked again this time a little calmer.

"First, you go to jail, then you leave off to God knows where with her and all the kids without calling me or anything. I mean you have been a real disappointment to me Case. Ever since you started dealing with that trash female, it's like I don't even know you." She sighed avoiding the question and letting me know without saying that it was true.

I had a body on me know, and a fucked-up head because she thought it would be in my best interest to have my girl ass beat until she damn near died.

I could only take so much disrespect from my mama. She had all this bullshit to say about Maliah but she never stopped to admit to herself that all the drama and problems we had now she was an accessory to. It was our family that was fuckin up Maliah's world not the other way around.

Just when I was about to give her a real piece of my mind uncut Nard walked into the living room. She instantly put her guard up higher after seeing him. He didn't open his mouth to speak to her and neither did she.

"I didn't know you were coming with him." She said to Nard with a rude tone

"Were you suppose to? When I come here it's not meant for anyone to know" He responded with a grin

Nard was a contracted hit man. Ever since we were kids he always talked about offing a muthafuckin, and it was my mama who saw fit for him to be used as a sniper. He never obliged because that's the path he was going to take anyway. In his entire 23 years of life he had countless bodies on him and had never been in custody for questioning. His fingerprints weren't even in the system; it was almost as if he only existed in *our* world. To say he was armed and dangerous would have been an understatement.

"Well how long will y'all be here?" She asked me after taking her attention from Nard

"However long it takes." He spat walking into the kitchen

The tension was so fuckin thick that I was beginning to feel uncomfortable and that wasn't a feeling that often overcame me.

"I want you to stay out of trouble, and if you knew like I knew then you would stay your ass here and not go back to wherever the hell she is" she warned.

I lost it after her remark, and her being my mother was not a factor at that point. I grabbed her by her neck and rammed her into the wall.

"If the only reason you came over here was to talk that shit then you're wasting yo' time. I have told you too many times not to over step yo' boundaries when it came to speaking on Maliah." I could see the fear plastered on her face, and it didn't faze me at all. She was cold and her true colors were showing.

"I came over here to see what was going on with Cailey and to see if you had spoken with Bridgette. You haven't been keeping me updated on nothing. I haven't talked to you in over a month, and then you call me to tell me that you're coming home for only a week." She cried hysterically.

"Get the fuck out of here I don't want to see you while I'm here, and once I go back home it's over for me talking to you. You took this shit too far, for no reason." I said

"Where is home at Case? I don't even know where you live at." She asked

I shook my head at her. She knew that was a question that wasn't going to get an answer. I wasn't telling a soul outside of Nard where my family was. I didn't trust her not to have Maliah hurt. She hated her so badly and I couldn't fathom why, which was a huge problem for me.

"I guess your whole world revolves around only her now. You shouldn't put all you have into one person, because when they're gone you will be left with nothing."

"What the fuck is that supposed to mean mama? She's next on y'all hit list? Anytime you can't control some shit you want it handled. You can take this how you want but she is a part of my family, and if you ever think about doing anything at all to hurt someone that I love, then you couldn't possibly care for or love me. It never ends well for people who purposely try to fuck with my livelihood." I stared at her so hard I could have burned a hole right through her.

"You heard the advice I just gave you Case. You will not keep bringing this family down with your nonsense and a bitch. The-."

"GET THE FUCK OUT! YOU DONE HERE!" I roared causing Nard to come out of the kitchen

"You can't disrespect me here; this is my house Casey Miller." She said

"Case chill out, you already know she's miserable as fuck and don't want to see anyone else happy." My brother said to me.

I could tell that she wanted to say something spiteful to Nard and she had a look plastered on her face as if it was painful for her to bite her tongue. That was the one person she walked light around. She knew that Nard didn't give a fuck about her and the only reason she probably was still breathing was because *I* loved her. He didn't have much of a heart and the little love he did show was the love for his brothers. He stood there wanting her to say something to set him off.

She looked us both up and down before storming out of the house. She always talked about me destroying the family name. It was already destroyed; *this dysfunctional ass family.*

Chapter 14: Maliah

After crying all night, I woke up to a wet pillow, my hair matted to my head, and a headache from over indulging in wine.

Cailey and Aden were both in the bed sleeping next to me. Over time they had become two peas in a pod. I searched my bed looking for my phone to find that Aden was lying on top of it. I had several misses calls and unread text from Casey. Most of his texts read that he arrived safely to Flint.

I eased out of bed with hopes of not waking either of them. When they were sleeping, the house was peaceful. The sun shined through the bay window nearly blinding me. I closed the curtained causing the room to go pitch black.

I stood in the bathroom mirror staring at how much of a mess my reflection was.
I proceeded to begin my daily hygiene regimen when I had the bright idea to board a plane back to Michigan.

Once Case came back home there was no way I would be able to go back. I had no family there so why I was so home sick I couldn't begin to try and figure out. I wanted to meet up with Shawnie and see if she had any leads on Eriq's death or maybe even my mothers. I couldn't keep up with the word in the streets living in Massachusetts, and if anything was traced back to Casey I was going to kill him no questions asked.

I needed to inform Marquita of my plan since she would be the one stuck at home with the kids. She wasn't going to be happy about it since she had plans for the weekend. It wasn't like we knew anyone here so either way she was going to be celebrating it with only us anyway.

As I walked into her room I took note of how perky her attitude was. She was just with the blues yesterday over Nard and now she was like a whole new woman.

"Why are you so happy?" I asked looking for an explanation

"What are you talking about?" she frowned at me for putting her on blast.

"You sitting in here with this big goofy smile on your face and I want to know why."

"I met someone, his name is Dontae. That's who I was hanging out with last night." She gushed cracking another smile.

I was excited and relieved that she wasn't in here smiling about Nard.

"He just texted me asking if I could come over for dinner next weekend. His dad and sister will be home." She smiled harder

"He must really like you, if he's introducing you to the family already." I smiled at her

"He's cool, he has the whole positive vibe thing going on. It's so weird because I was not trying to give him a chance when I met him. I thought he was ugly." She laughed

"Good, I'm happy for you! Why would you think he was ugly? Is he ugly?" I asked.

"No not at all, but he looks so familiar. Clearly I don't know him or anyone else out here, but I feel like I've seen him before somewhere." She said in deep thought

"You're just picky that's all, I hope he sticks around longer than a week. Sooo, I am thinking about leaving to go to Michigan tonight." I told her changing the subject

"Michigan? But Case said he didn't want us going there anytime soon" she replied sounding like she was programmed by Case.

"Girl, fuck what Case said. I'm going" her telling me what I was told not to do only made me solidify my plan on leaving.

"I'm leaving tonight and I'll be back in two days." I told her

"But what about my plans? I have a date." She whined

"They can stay home with Ms. James and Jaylen for a few hours."

"Alright if you insist, but you better be careful." She said

I wasn't announcing that I would be coming back in town I wanted it to be unexpected. I sat at my dining room table making reservations for my flight and hotel room. I also decided to add a car rental so I could get around.

All that day I ensured that the kids had everything they would need in my absence. I didn't want to leave them but I would be back before they knew I was gone. My flight was scheduled to take off late that way it was after Ms. James's shift. I didn't need her blowing my cover by calling Case and informing him of my arrival. I wanted it to be a surprise for everyone. I didn't have time for that shit.

My land line rang indicating that someone was at the gate. I viewed the security camera to see who it was because I wasn't expecting anyone. There sat a young guy in an Aston Martin DB9. I had no idea who he was so I went to ask Marquita.

"Hey do you know who this is at the gate?" Without responding she turned on her TV to view the security camera.

"Yea that's Dontae," she said hopping out the bed racing to the mirror to fix her hair.

"He drives an Ashton Martin, and his name is Dontae Carleone?" I couldn't help but to ask, I didn't want to pass judgement but it sounded like he was a street nigga to me.

"His dad is filthy fuckin rich, and yes, his real last name is Carleone." She said in his defense. She knew me too well to know where my thoughts were leading to.

"Interesting." was all that I managed to say. I walked down to the foyer with her eager to meet the mystery man that had my sister on a natural high.

She opened the door and in walked this 6'3 pretty boy. I was expecting him to be ugly since she told me that was her first impression of him. Not only was he not ugly in fact he didn't have one ugly feature. His long dreads were neatly twisted and down his back with a perfect line up. The smile he was giving us was bright with perfect shining teeth.

He possessed a baby face, and couldn't have been older than 18.

"Dontae this is my sister Maliah, Maliah this is Dontae Carleone." She introduced us

"Pleasure to meet you Maliah." He said in the most adorable Boston accent ever.

Marquita was right he did look very familiar, and I was going to beat myself over the head trying figure out where did we know him from. My guess was we didn't know him, but he had a look alike from somewhere; probably a celebrity look alike or some shit.

"Nice meeting you as well." I smiled to him.

Marquita escorted him to the family room where all the kids were. I was hoping the forces were with him. The kids hadn't seen a new face outside of Ms. James in months and they were about to question that man to death.

I packed my bags while listening to Jhene Aiko's *Promises*

Everything is alright, everything's in your mind
Life is what you make it, life is what you make it
And anything can happen, anything can happen
But you just gotta get past it, you just gotta laugh at it
Anything can happen, you fall down get back up
And you better believe that nothing holding me back
So everything is alright, everything is alright
Everything is alright, promise I'll be
Promise you'll be, promise we'll be alright

Listening to her lyrics had tears falling rapidly from my eyes. I missed my mama, and I missed Eriq.

I wished that it was something that I would have could do for the both to save their lives.

If I could have let my mama know more of what I needed from her, and that I loved her then maybe she would still have been here. If could have held Eriq's hand tighter as those bullets filled his body, then maybe he would have fought harder to survive. Although deep down in my heart I knew that the both of their deaths were far beyond my control. I still had guilt on my conscious. I often wondered how my life would be now if Eriq would have never left with my money or if my relationship with Casey never happened.

My phone vibrated on the dresser snapping me back to the reality of it all.
Casey's name appeared across the screen. I took a deep breath before answering.

"Hello."

"Wassup, how are you?" he asked I hadn't responded to his text so I knew it was only a matter of time before he called me

"I'm fine, just organizing my clothes." I left out the part about organizing them because I was packing and heading to where he was.

"Where are the kids, how are they?" he asked in a suspicious tone

"They're down stairs in the family room watching a movie." I responded

"They love their damn movies man, I miss y'all. It won't be long before I'm back and we can put all of this behind us finally."

"I'm hoping that we can Casey, it's been a long road. So, some type of closure needs to happen and fast." I sighed

"Maliah, I know shit has been fucked up for you, shit for us.... but I want you to know that my only intention from the day I saw you sitting in that diner was to be a good nigga for you. I know we experienced some twists and turns but if that's everything that had to happen for it be us in the end I wouldn't have it no other way for real." he admitted

I took a long pause to process everything that he was saying to. His words had me second guessing my decision to go back home. It was no denying that I loved him and I would choose him over and over again. The problem was my heart wouldn't allow me to be satisfied with his word on not being associated with the deaths that hit so close to home for me.

"I love you Casey, I really do. I need time to heal, to grow, and to let go of a lot of things that has happened to me in my life that I am still holding on to. You must give me time, because right now I'm good to myself so I can't be good to you or anyone else. I'm too broken." I cried

"I love you too. I'll give you all the time that you need, but I'm not going anywhere. I'm here for you. Stop crying and do something to make yourself feel a little better. Go spend all of my money that always made you happy." He laughed to lighten the conversation

He always managed to make me laugh, if he couldn't do anything else he could make me laugh.

"Bye, I don't know what you're talking about." I laughed

I stared at the suitcase sitting on my bed. I hated to go behind his back, but I had to look out for myself. I continued to finish packing because according to the clock I had less than 3 hours to make it to the airport.

I was heading back to Flint and I was coming for answers.

Chapter 15: Bridgette

"Move the fuck over!!" I yelled at the top of my lungs to at Roc

He was a bum from around my mama's neighborhood that I was using temporarily to help cope with the excruciating pain my heart was feeling. I had been laying up in his spot smoking and drinking the day away. This was an ongoing routine since I came back to Chicago. I left here years ago because I wanted to escape my problems. When I left, and moved to Detroit I promised myself I was never coming back. After I met Case and later moved to Flint with him I just knew for sure I wasn't coming back.

My life was perfect. I had met a fine ass man that came from wealth with a good heart, I was the baddest chick around and we were living the life together. I didn't need shit else.

All that changed when he met this bitch Maliah. She ruined our fuckin future together, and now she had *my* daughter after taking *my* man. I couldn't deal with it. Every time I thought about it I found myself in the bottom of a bottle of some cheap ass liquor or smoking some shaky weed.

I lost everything. After I left with Cailey Case stopped paying my mortgage causing my condo to go into foreclosure. I was only trying to wake him up so he could see what he was missing with me. I wasn't expecting him to stop paying all my bills leaving me with nothing.

My mama was completely cut the fuck off for reaching out to Maliah behind my back. I wasn't attending her funeral after cancer was through with her ass.

"You go watch how you talk to me or you can get the fuck out." Roc warned standing up and pointing to the door

I wanted to tell him that I would be glad to get out of the small, dirty ass apartment he lived in but it was the only place I had to go. I didn't have two dollars to my name to go anyplace else. So, I had to stay in good with his dirt ball ass.

"I was saying daddy you can't hog the entire bed." I said in a nicer tone to him
Sleeping with his fat ass in this full-size bed was becoming to be too much; something had to shake fast.

"Good bitch you better say it in a much better tone." He got back in the bed and began to rub his tiny dick on my leg. I rolled my eyes up to the ceiling. I was not in the mood to pretend to enjoy sex with him. I just wanted him to leave me the fuck alone while I put a plan together to leave this hell hole.

"Come over here." He instructed

I slowly sat up and moved in closer to him. I looked at the sight of him and felt discussed. Everything about his fat sloppy body, musty body odor, and his small penis that he was thumbing made me want to puke. I didn't have to get undressed because I was fucking his jack rabbit ass every time I looked up so I never had clothes on.

I sat on him and straddled what felt like nothing, closed my eyes and pretended he was Case like I had done each time.

There was no follow up to replace him. Case was the man when it came to everything, you couldn't get closer to perfect than him even if you put 5 niggas together. It wasn't happening. I got sick at the thought of me never feeling his touch again.

Tears begin to stream down my face unwillingly. I quickly used the back of my hand to wipe them away. Before I could clear my face of all tears Roc's open hand connected with my face.

"You thinkin' about that nigga again?!! He yelled

I began to cry even harder, not because Roc hit me, but because I missed Case. I didn't care what happened to me if I couldn't have him. My world revolved around him. If I wasn't so afraid of letting go of the hope that maybe one day we would be together again I would kill myself. I would sit in the local library and leave numerous messages in Maliah's Facebook inbox threatening to kill myself if they didn't bring me back Cailey. She never responded to any of my messages.

"I wasn't thinking about him Roc!" I screamed at him

"I'm sick of your shit Bridgette, you better get your muthafuckin mind together if you go be livin in my shit. Do you understand me?!" He scolded

I nodded my head yes as I watched him put his clothes back on. Like clockwork every day he had to go play his lottery.

"When I come back you're going to finish this job off with a smile on your face." He said pointing down at his dick. Once I was back with Case and this was all behind me I was going to kill his fat ass for treating me like this. It couldn't be anything worse than a broke, dirty ass nigga that thought you were within their favor.

As soon as the door closed I jumped up out of the bed and put my clothes on and ran over to his little money stash that he saved up weekly to buy prescription drugs off the streets to use. I fumbled through the money and it was a total of $220.00 in the drawer.

I shook my head at how broke this nigga was. This wasn't enough money to fly back to Michigan. This was barely enough money to catch a catch a cab around the city.
Fuck.

Refusing to give up hope, I still took the money, hurried to my car and sped off in the opposite direction of the store where Roc was. I stopped by the gas station to gas up my car, and buy me a minute phone. I didn't have much time to get the fuck on because Roc would be on my ass and ready to kill me over this little money. I drove my car onto 94 East back to Flint. I called Mrs. Rice, it had been a while since I spoke with her. My phone had been turned off after Case stopped paying my bill. I wasn't sure if she had the same number but I was going to try it. I had no place to go when I got there and I knew that she would open her doors to me.

"Hello?" Mrs. Rice answered

"Hey Ma, it's me Bridgette" I nervously spoke

"Girl where the hell are you!?" She yelled with concern

"I'm on my way back to Flint now, can I come stay with you? I'll only be in town for the week." I lied

I couldn't tell her everything that I was going through because I didn't want it to get back to Case.

"Of course you can come here, my door is always open for you!" she shouted with excitement.

"Thanks, Ma. I knew that I can always count on you. I'll be there later this evening." I said grateful for her hospitality.

"Okay baby, I'll see you later."

I was going to get my man and daughter back even if it meant taking down whoever was standing in my way.

Chapter 16: Case

I stood in the mirror admiring myself in my Giorgio Armani tailored suit. Tonight, Gino was in town and whenever he came home we held a family meeting and party. Those meetings always took place in an upscale restaurant where he reserves to host the private event. These meetings have taken place for years but this one I was eager to attend so I could question him regarding his affiliation to all the incidents that occurred.

We were also putting our plan into effect to have Eriq's brothers taken care of. Once everything was handled it was safe for me to say that I was done with Flint, Michigan because being home no longer felt good to me. I couldn't trust my family, and I was looking over my shoulder with every step that I took. It wasn't a good feeling to have and I was over it all.

"Nigga you looking spiffy" I joked with Nard. He walked out of the bedroom looking like he stepped off a runway. He hardly ever attended the meetings or the parties so seeing him suited up was rare.

"I can pull so many bitches off this look here." He laughed stretching his arms out and admiring his apperarance.

"Yo', I'm telling you now if they get to talking shit at this lil shindig I'm out of there. I don't have time to hear the okie doke from them. That's the shit they do that makes me distance myself." He mumbled to himself.

"I'm where you are mentally with that too bro. They stay sweeping shit under the rug and playing on muthafucka's intelligence and it's over for. I'm at the point where I will stay tucked off with my family and never fuck with them again. I'm tired of them thinking that family is only about running an organization." I fumed

"Exactly." Nard Mumbled

We rode together to the restaurant in an all-black Suburban. The directions to the location of the event were never given until a half hour before it began for security purposes. Although extended family joined in, at some time during the night our immediate family would talk about what's going on, and we would then learn Gino's next move.

The meeting was far on the other side of town and we were stuck in traffic. I used this as an opportunity to check in on Maliah. She wasn't texting me back as fast as I would have liked her to. I figured she was sleeping since when I spoke with her earlier her spirit was down. Again, no answer from her. I decided to call Marquita to see if everything was okay.

"Hey Bro" she answered into the phone on the first ring

"Wassup, what's going on over there? Everything alright?" I asked

"Yea everything is cool, the kids are getting ready for bed, and I'm on the phone right now."

"Where is your sister? She's not answering?" I questioned her

"She was upstairs in the room. I'm not sure if she's sleeping or not. I'll check and hit you back." She said rushing me off the phone. I'm sure the phone call she was on wasn't an important one.

"Alright, make sure you tell her to hit me back." I instructed

With the way traffic was flowing we were guaranteed to be late.

"Damn this shit is crazy" Nard said hitting the steering wheel.

Here I was stuck in a car again with his ole impatient ass. He had me wishing I would have taken a couple of shots before I left the crib.

Finally, we made it to our destination without being as late as I thought we would be. I spotted a few familiar cars in the parking lot. With no hesitation, I got out of the car because I couldn't wait to get this shit over with. I secured my 9mm hand gun under my suit jacket, and proceeded to enter the restaurant. Nard decided to stay in the car for a moment to smoke a blunt. Dealing with our parents wasn't easy and with the temper that Nard possessed made it twice as hard for him to be civil.

The moment I walked into the restaurant I was greeted by my father's security team.

"Good seeing you Case, it's been a minute." Lorenzo said to me.

He worked for my dad as his head of security since I was in diapers. It was always a pleasure to see Lorenzo, he had aged a bit and it wouldn't be much longer before he was coming out for retirement.

"It's good seeing you as well Lorenzo." I firmly shook his hand. I wasn't searched by security so it wasn't long before I was walking into the grand dining room where my mama was sitting on one end of the table and my dad on the other. After the altercation with my mama I didn't want to say shit to her, but I was raised better than to be disrespectful so I embraced her with a hug.

Her vibe was off as usual, she seemed to be nervous but I blew it off as her just being her. My dad stood up to hug me before I prepared to take my seat next to him when I thought my eyes were playing tricks on me. Bridgette was walking toward the table in a long fitted gold gown. Her hair was pinned up in a bun and for the first time ever she was out in public with no makeup on. Her bare face looked a lot better than it did with all the makeup she wore. Although she looked beautiful I was steaming with rage that she was there.

"Did I miss the fuckin memo or what?" I asked staring at my mama for an explanation.

"Not right now Case, it's not what you think, I'll tell you about it later." She whispered

Tell me about it later.

It made no sense to me that she was in my space. I still wanted to break her face for leaving with Cailey. It wasn't a good idea for her to be in my presence right now.

If it wasn't for me needing to talk to my pops I would have left right, then and there. I flagged down the waiter and instructed for him to bring me a shot of Hennessy. I needed something to relax me because every glance I took at Bridgette made my blood pressure rise. She knew that she fucked up because she didn't even speak to me. I could tell that she wanted to but her ass knew better. Just then Nard joined us at the table. He immediately noticed Bridgette because he wasted no time speaking on it.

"What is going on here? He asked

"Nard take a seat, we're all family here." She said

"Yea sure" he said sarcastically

If Bridgette wanted to play these types of games and be close to my family, I was going to do something that was going to hurt her the most.

I was going to ignore her ass until it was time for me to leave. The one thing that I had to keep in mind when it came to her was the fact she was my daughter's mama. I had to deal with her for the rest of my life and that was the consequence I had to pay for fuckin with her crazy ass in the first place. The signs were there a long time ago. As far as my mama I was going to handle her. She knew about all the bullshit that Bridgette had just put me through with Cailey but that didn't stop her from still bringing her into my space without telling me what was going on first. Her loyalty was with not Bridgette; it should have been with me *her son.*

"It's good everyone made it here safe and sound." My dad said in his deep Barry White voice.

Everyone nodded their head in agreement with him while placing dinner orders with the waiters. Bridgette sat several seats down and across the table from me but I could feel her staring at me. I had to get the fuck from out of there before I lost it.

"Pops, can we holla at you for a minute?" I asked him

"After dinner please, I haven't had shit to eat all day." He groaned

"It'll only take a minute; I'll make it quick before your food even gets here." I pushed

He stood up out of his seat while Nard and I followed his lead. He walked toward the back of the restaurant and into an empty back office.

"What is it that couldn't hold off until after I ate something" he complained

"I want to know what went down with all the shit that took place with Rosie." I asked him getting straight to the point

He took a long dramatic huff to let me know that he thought that I was wasting his time. The organization he ran had been going strong for over 20 years and here I was talking to him about a stealing crackhead. Even I would have thought I was being ridiculous if it wasn't Maliah's mother I was talking about.

"Listen son, I don't know how serious the attachment was to this Rosie lady you had, but she stole from me. Not on one occasion but two." He said holding up two fingers to exaggerate his point.

"When you steal drugs or anything from someone you better believe it's a price to pay. Now I did take you into consideration because I called off several hits on her, but we had another issue...she wouldn't shut the hell up. Not only did she steal, she had to brag about it all over the city. Now I had people questioning was it true, and police sniffing at my door step. What's a man left to do? Kill the bitch right son?" He rhetorically asked me.

I was aware of how the streets was, and I guess my only reason for coming to him with this was because I wanted him to tell me that he had nothing to do with her dying and that it was due to a drug overdose. He confirmed what I wanted to know. It wasn't a drug overdose, she was killed. And it was my family that killed her off. It was definite that I had to let Maliah go, I couldn't carry knowing that information and continuing to lie to her. I was better off not knowing and really giving her my truth that I didn't know.

I wasn't upset with my dad because he did what he had to do to protect his empire. My love life wasn't going to be his downfall. As fucked up as it was I understood his decision, but I would never ask Maliah to try to understand. My dad must have saw the pain his information caused me because he did something he hadn't done since I was a kid; he hugged me.

Nard hung his head down because he knew better than anyone how much I loved Maliah and I wanted to make this work someway, somehow.

"The food has been served." My little cousin Asia informed us

I straightened out my suit jacket and dust the chip off my shoulder as I joined my family for dinner. My drink order request was in full rotation. I needed to succumb from the pain that I felt in my heart and liquor would assist me with that.

Everyone was mingling and pretending to be this normal ass family. When the truth was, my family was the furthest thing from normal. I stood by the window looking through my phone. Maliah or Marquita had not called me back and that was weighing heavily on my mind.

"Hey, can I talk to you?" Bridgette asked creeping up behind me

"Man, get the fuck away from me." I was going through enough emotions inside and her presence was not needed to make it worse.

"I just want to talk for 5 minutes about the way I went about things Case. I want to apologize to you." She sighed

"You can keep your apologies Bridgette; I don't want to talk to you." I could feel myself getting angry about the stunt she pulled all over again and she needed to get the fuck on.

"I'm sorry Case, I've been dealing with depression and heartbreak. I don't know how to live without you." She admitted with tears running down her face.

Here she goes with this shit.

"I don't care about your heartbreak or depression, you left with my child. If it wasn't for your mama telling us how shitty of a mother, you were I would still be tossing and turning not knowing where my baby was. Fuck you" I spat with venom

It was nothing she could say to make me feel sorry for her or to forgive her. I was literally sick not knowing where this bitch was with Cailey. All because she was hurt that I didn't want her anymore. My choices on stringing her along weren't cool, but you don't seek revenge by using my baby. That wasn't a wise choice for her. Little did she know that she made it hard for herself not only could she not have me; she would never have custody of Cailey for as long as she lived.

"So you really don't care huh? It's really over?" She asked me

I didn't know how many more actions I had to take, or how many more hurtful words I had to say for her to get it.

"It is over, I have nothing at all in my heart for you. The love I did have for you as Cailey's mother is gone. Now I would appreciate if you got out away from me." I said coldly.

She stopped crying and began to smile as if I didn't just say anything at all to her. She was nuts out of her mind.

"I know you don't mean that, it's always been us Case. I'm just waiting for you to see that we are meant to be together and the feelings that you have for Maliah are just a phase."

Her crazy ass went on to talk about our history together but all her words trailed off when I saw Shawnie and Maliah heading my way like mad black women.

Oh, shit

I thought my eyes were playing tricks on me. There was no way Maliah was here at my family's meeting. I left her in Massachusetts, so I couldn't process the idea of her being here. The closer she got to me the more my heart thumped harder in my chest. She has on a long red gown, and her long hair flowed as she walked. The lights glowed off her face; she was beautiful even with the mean mug that she had on her face. I felt like the devil himself was coming after me. There was no doubt in my mind that the shit was about to hit the fan, and I did not want to be in this building. She was in full beast mode and my ass better thought quickly if I wanted to avoid her raft.

"YOU LEFT ME, TO COME TO DINNER WITH THIS BITCH?!!!! She yelled at the top of her lungs not giving a fuck that my entire family was in the same room.

"Baby, no! I had no idea she would be here." I said fumbling for words. I was pissed Bridgette was standing there smiling. I wanted to slap that fuckin smile off her face. The hoe was ruining my life right along with my crazy ass mama.

This was not a good look for me, I looked like I was lying my ass off the way Bridgette and me was tucked off in this dark ass corner.

"You keep trying to play me, I'm home with all those damn kids and you here back home living" she cried swinging at me wildly. I caught her hand blocking her punch causing her to get angrier, at that point I thought I would be better off just letting her punches connect.

"I'm so tired of you Casey, you and this hoe!! " she screamed kicking her shoes off to charge at Bridgette, but her scary ass ran from Maliah and slid next to my mama. I grabbed Maliah to keep her from beating Bridgette's ass. It wasn't that I didn't want her to get her ass beat, I just couldn't have Maliah out here fighting anyone, especially in this situation. I was not on no bullshit and she needed to know that I was an innocent man. She fought me to let her go but I snatched her up and took her to the back office where I was talking to my dad earlier.

"I can't believe you, I really can't fuckin believe you! You keep making a fool out of me. I came here with hopes of being wrong but what did I find!!?" She sat in the office chair and cried.

There was not one thing that I could tell her to make her believe me. What she saw was me and my baby mama dressed up, tucked off from everyone else in a restaurant with my family, while she was left at home. I was mad at my mama; it was her fault for bringing Bridgette here in the first fuckin place.

"You really don't give a fuck Casey, yo' tired ass was all on my phone in my ear telling me how you love me and will be waiting on me but you fuckin me over behind my back. No wonder why yo' ass wanted me out of Flint so bad. The both of you deserve each other, two sad ass people together." She went on and on tearing a nigga down. I just stood there and let her words soak in, I was innocent but it didn't mean a thing in this present moment.

"Maliah, I'm being so honest with you right now. My mama invited her here like she always does. She was over there trying to talk to me but it was nothing like what you are thinking right now." I pleaded

I wanted her to hear me out, but I also wanted to ask her why in the hell was she here, after I told her numerous times that she wasn't allowed back in this city. I had a mission that I had to be on tonight and I didn't need her in the mist of gunfire.

"I don't know why I came here, I already know all the answers I need to know to cancel you out of my life for good. You came into my life like you were so much better than what I was use to and honestly I would much rather be back in my small ass townhouse, stressing over where Eriq is than here amongst you and your family full of drug dealers and killers."

Her words cut me deep, mostly because I felt the same way. The outcome with Rosie wouldn't have been much different but at the same time she wouldn't be sitting with the people who were responsible for killing her mother.

"You deserve better than everything that you've been going through. I think it would be best if you took care of yourself and got you together, but not here." I stressed

I didn't care what the fuck she was talking about her days in Flint were over as long as I was still breathing.

"You know Casey, that's what I don't like about you. You like to control shit; you think that you can tell me what I'm not going to do even after we are over and done. It's not going to happen. I'm going to live where I chose to." She argued

I still openly let her words soak in, she was right I couldn't control what she decided to do after me.

"Where are you staying tonight? Do you mind me asking that?" I wanted nothing more than for her to get on a plane tonight and go home but I knew that was highly unlikely to happen.

"I'm going to Shawnie's house tonight, when I go back to Massachusetts it will be to get the kids." She emphasized.

Just as I was leaving out of the office Bridgette came walking in.

"Before you say anything crazy Case I just want to get something off my chest." Bridgette said

"I don't want to hear shit you have to say bitch." Maliah gritted

"Would you shut the fuck and listen! Damn!" Bridgette yelled rolling her eyes

Maliah stood up out of the chair she was sitting in to get into attack mode again.

"I don't have to listen to shit you have to say, I'm sick of your bullshit, and your stunts that you pull. What you need to know is that I don't give a fuck about you and Casey is not a concern of mine either." She rebut

What Maliah didn't know was that she was wrong. I was willing to let her have some space to get her mind right but she was far from being a free agent.

"If you're going to be in Cailey's life you need to be able to be civil with me since I am her mother." Bridgette smiled. She was probably doing back flips mentally after hearing Maliah confess that we were over.

"Let's be real you don't care about Cailey, you used your own child to try to keep a nigga, one who doesn't even want you, you are fuckin pitiful, and I'm done here. There is no need for me to continue to waste my time. The both of you are truly made for each other." Just as Maliah finished getting her feelings off her chest my mama walked into the office.

Man, what the fuck. These crazy ass females were not about to drive me crazy. I had enough stress for one night.

"Why are you here Maliah? I thought you were somewhere safe, where my son had you hidden." My mama asked in a sarcastic tone.

"You and her need to mind your business and go back out there to tend to your guest." I said to her and referring to Bridgette.

"Mind my business? Boy, you are my business." My mama argued

"No, that's where you are sadly mistaken Mrs. Rice. Casey is not your business, and the sooner you realize that the better off you would fuckin be. He is a grown ass man with his own responsibilities. You have done enough damage to *our* lives" Maliah said snaking her neck

"You little bitch-" my mama never finished what she was about to say because I intervened.

"All of y'all need to get the out of here, now!! I'm sick of all this shit between the 3 of you it's pointless as hell. Bridgette, you need to go back to where the fuck you came from. Maliah you're taking your ass home" I looked at my mama without knowing what to tell her. I was only there for one reason and that was to talk to Gino. After Ayesha informed me that my own mother was behind all the foul play I officially had to write her off. And I wasn't changing mind. It was her who taught me that an untrustworthy person couldn't be trusted as far as you could see them and even then, they were deceitful.

Bridgette folded her arms and poked her lip out like she was six years old.

"And yo' ass is too damn old to be so childish. Go...now!" I yelled at my mama as I pointed to the door and they all pouted on their way out.

Maliah wasted no time pulling on Shawnie's arm to leave the building.

"Bridgette you need to take your ass home, wherever the fuck that is." I laughed. I told her when she pregnant with Cailey that I was going to always do what was necessary to make sure that she was taken care of, but since she pulled that stunt and took her away from me I was happy to shut down everything I paid for her.

"Home is with yo' mama" she smirked at me

Her words hit me like a ton of bricks. *I know she just didn't tell me that she was staying with my mama.*

"What did you just say?" I wanted to hear her wrong.

"I'm staying with your mother Case until I can get settled back here...at home." She mumbled

My eyes roamed the restaurant until they landed on my mama. She was causing me more drama than what my life needed. The betrayal with her was getting to be very real. There was no way that she had all this animosity towards Maliah that she was willing to make *my* life a living hell. It had to have been more to her story of Maliah just simply not being good enough for me. I was no walking saint and she knew that shit better than anyone.

I was going to check her ass about her going behind my again, but I needed to catch up with Shawnie and Maliah to see where they were off to. I didn't want her to be so mad at me that she forgot that she was wanted in these streets.

I grabbed her arm only for her to pull away from me.

"I want you to leave me alone Casey, why is that so damn hard for you to comprehend. I don't want you to worry about me, my safety or any of the above!!" she yelled.

I nodded my head and threw my hands up to indicate that I was surrendering to her request. It would be hard but I knew that the more that I pushed she would pull away from me and I could understand why after considering all that she had been through.

I made my way back into the restaurant to find my mama.

"Yo', what made you think it was okay to bring Bridgette here and then have her living with you?" I fumed

"She is my grandchild's mother Case. She shouldn't need a place to live with all the money you have! You ought to be ashamed of yourself." she said cutting her eyes at me.

I never had the urge to disrespect my mama as much as I had since I arrived back in this city but with passing time I was losing respect more and more.

"When she decided to take my daughter away from me it was fuck her and if you ain't with me on that then it's fuck you!" I said walking away from her and to the exit.

"That little bitch has your head gone, I wonder what you go do when she leaves you for the next!!" She screamed

I signaled for Nard to leave with me when he told me that he was leaving with our pops. I was opposed to going back to my mama's spot, because I didn't need her popping up on with more of her bullshit.

I tried calling Maliah only for her phone to go straight to voicemail.

"Fuck" I shouted hitting the steering wheel. I hated to be out of control of situations and in this moment, I was very out of control. I drove to Shawnie's house to have a face to face conversation with Maliah since I couldn't talk to her over the phone.

When I got to Shawnie's house her Nissan wasn't in the driveway. I was pissed that I had driven that far out to see her house and they weren't there.

I decided to call Shawnie to see where they were but she didn't answer my call. I walked up the pavement that lead to her front door. I was about to bang that muthafucka down or sit on the porch until they got there. Maliah had me fucked up if she thought I was about to let her roam this city with niggas after her head. I banged on Shawnie's door until she answered it.

She came to the door with her hair a mess all over her head, and some big, bald headed nigga standing behind her.

"Man, where fuck is Maliah at?" I asked mugging the nigga since he wanted to come to the door like he owned some shit.

"She went to the store Case, she ain't even been gone 5 minutes." She said looking at her watch.

"Why would you let her go to the store this at this time of night by herself, knowing the amount of drama she's in." I asked taking my phone out of my pocket to call her again.

I was growing anxious. I don't know why she couldn't have just stayed her hard-headed ass back in Massachusetts. I hadn't gotten shit accomplished since I got back to the city because of these messy ass females that I had around me.

I shook my head out of frustration.

"Ayo, let me fuck up in here." I said opening the door wider so that I could barge right in.

I sat on the couch and retrieved my gun from my hip and sat it on my lap. I had so much tension and anger bottled up inside that if this nigga breathed too loud I was going to empty a clip in him.

"I'll be back there in a minute let me just talk to my cousin for a minute." Shawnie said to him

He went back to the room like she had told him to do.

"What do you mean let her Case? You out of all people know there is no letting her do anything once she has her mind made up that's what's she's doing. She will back the store is two minutes up the street." She tried to reason with me but wasn't hearing her. It only took a bullet .5 second to kill someone. So, I wasn't trying to hear that 2-minute store run shit. I wasn't leaving her fuckin couch until Maliah brought her ass back.

Chapter 17: Maliah

I sat in the Shawnie's parked car at a gas station pump with tears streaming from my eyes while my heart burned and my eyes stung. Casey didn't expect me to be in town and he was back to his usual ways, playing games and still hanging on to his baby mama.

What hurt me the most was that I was now facing the music, he and I were over. There wasn't anything to salvage together. Me coming to Michigan was about finding out the truth and I wasn't here a full 24 hours before running into Casey being on some bullshit.

I felt like I was tricked from day 1 with him because I had all the reasons in the world to believe that he never genuinely had good intentions for me from the start. Although I was back home I knew that this was not home the streets didn't feel safe and overall I felt like I was a target. I wasn't sure if it was the stories that Shawnie was telling me about how my name was the topic of every conversation or what but I didn't like it. I didn't like it one bit.

I got out of the car to grab me a juice to mix with the liquor I had waiting on me at Shawnie's. I was about to drown out in the bottle tonight and celebrate my new-found freedom, a life without *Casey*. After paying for my juice I walked out to the car and I was only within a 4-foot range of the car when my body froze when the touch of metal barrel pressed up against my spine shocked me.

"Walk over to that blue van or else your back is about to be blasted." A guy said with venom pouring off his tongue.

Rather if I walked over to the van or decided to run he was going to kill me anyway. I could tell by how cold his tone was that he was waiting to run into me like this. His hands trembled as the gun vibrated on my lower back. I was nervous that he was shaking. I was once told that if a person with a gun was shaking it was an indicator that they were liable to shoot just off being nervous.

I slowly walked towards the van before I decided to make a run for it. I ran towards the curb but that was as far as I made it before a white Chrysler Sebring stopped in front me and a masked man jumped out of the car from the passenger's side.

The man who initially had the gun to me caught up and hit me in my face with the butt of his gun causing a dizzy spell to overcome me instantly.

"Stupid ass bitch" he grunted highly frustrated that I had ran. His words echoed as I slipped in and out of consciousness.

Against my will they picked me up and placed me in the back seat of the car. I tried to kick and scream but everything was in slow motion.

The same guy that hoped out of the passenger's side took his mask off and turned around to look at me. It was Sam, Eriq's brother. Casey had been warning me about him being on the prowl for me, but I was stupid enough to believe that with the history that Sam and I had there wouldn't be these type of problems. I was sadly mistaken because the nigga had just abducted me. As I went to open my mouth a piece of duct tape was strapped across it by the person sitting next to me.

The excruciating pain from the blow I took when he hit me with the gun was too much to bare. I laid back on the seat and closed my eyes praying to die so that I could escape the pain I was feeling and the possible torture I was getting ready to undergo. I had a glimmer of hope that Casey would save me, but I couldn't dwell on the idea of that happening.

I woke up to ice cold water being dumped on my head. I wasn't aware that I had fallen asleep. While I was sleeping my hands were tied up and so were my feet. My body stiffened as the cold water attack my skin. The migraine that I was experiencing had me seeing double. I was sitting on a dirty basement floor with two men standing over me. The one that douched me with water threw the bucket aggressively cross the room causing me to be more alert.

I felt hands fondling my ass and it caused me to jump out of shock. I didn't want to be sexually assaulted I would have rather died than to be raped.

"Nigga, stop! Stick to what we are doing." A familiar voice said to my assailant.

I focused my eyes on the faces before me and it was Sam and his brother Tate. I had forgotten that my mouth was covered with tape until it was snatched off by Tate. For a split second the pain from my migraine had been trumped by the pain of having the skin on my lips ripped off.

I was disgusted that Tate was willing to rape me. I met him before I met Eriq but I shot him down because he wasn't my type and I guess that he still felt some type of way about it.

"I had nothing to do with what happened to Eriq" I groaned.

The both looked at each other and shook their heads.

"Do you think we're fuckin stupid?? You were with him, in the same car and you ain't get hit. Not once!!!" Sam yelled at me while kneeling down so that we were face to face with only a few inches between us.

Before I said another word, I sat up against the wall and contemplated my word choice. What he was saying pointed to me being suspect, but I had to prove to them that I was innocent if I wanted to walk out this shit alive.

"You should have stayed yo' ass where ever the fuck you were hiding out at, because I ain't hearing shit you saying. Tate said dismissing my argument before I had opportunity to give me side of the story.

"I came here to talk to y'all, and find out who fuckin killed Eriq. I had nothing to do with it. I'm just as curious as you are to know why I walked away." I explained as I winced in pain.

I glanced over by the stairway to await the footsteps that were beginning to trail down to where we were. Once the footsteps stopped appeared a fat chubby nigga and Mrs. Rice. My eyes bulged at the sight of her. *Why is she here.* As much as she hated me I still had hopes that maybe she was here to save me.

"Nigga not now! I'm in the middle of handling some shit and why the fuck are you bringing bitches here??!" Sam yelled at the pudgy guy.

I had no idea what the fuck was going on but I needed answers now.

"Bitch? You have no idea who I am Samuel? You've been working for me for almost 2 years now, you don't know him bringing me here wasn't much of an option?" Mrs. Rice asked pulling a gun out of her purse.

"Work for you? Nah... get the fuck out of here. I'll deal with you later." Sam said waving her off and redirecting his attention to me.

POW POW POW

Three shots rang off all connecting with Sam's head. I flinched as his body crashed to the floor and landing only a few feet away from where I was sitting. Tate drew his gun in Mrs. Rice's direction but not in enough time to beat the bullets that filled his body from gun that chubby nigga has in hand while leaving his lifeless body to fall on top of Sam's.

I closed my eyes thinking that if I opened them again I would be someplace safe.

"Shit is crazy Shuck...all his dumb ass had to do was listen." Mrs. Rice said to Chubbs.

"I came here when I got word that you were kidnapped Maliah, kidnapped without *my* permission. I don't know if I came to actually save you or witness you suffering." She smiled at me.

"You are one sick ass woman. You're supposed to be a mother and a wife and you're just a dirty-

I didn't get to finish my sentence because the bitch shot at the wall only a few inches from my head. I no longer cared at this point. If my mercy lied in the hands of this evil ass woman, then I wasn't going to go out with my tail between my legs. It was fuck her and everything she stood for.

"Shut the fuck up, I like the idea of you suffering. You talk too fuckin much." She snapped

I just couldn't understand why she hated my guts, and the air I breathed and I the only thing I had done was love her disloyal ass son. She placed the tape that covered my mouth before from the dirty ass floor and placed it back over my mouth. If I made it out of this basement I made a promise to myself that I was going to kill this bitch myself.

She walked over to the light switch and turned the lights out leaving me sitting there tied up with two dead bodies in the dark.

"Let's see if you can get yourself out of this situation." She laughed walking up the stairs with the fat nigga in tow.

I said a silent prayer to myself as warm tears fell from my eyes. I would have rather her shot me than me to having to endure the turmoil I was getting ready to face.

Chapter 18: Marquita

"Yo', you don't hear her crying?" Jaylen asked me.

All my attention was focused in on the texts that Dontae were sending me. He had just left my house, but the way I was blushing you would have thought that I hadn't talked to him in years. He was so different than the guys that I usually talked to. He was the opposite of the streets and what was weird was that the same reasons I liked him were the exact opposite of why I liked Nard.

"No I didn't hear her crying" I responded to Jaylen who was holding Cailey in his arms.

"That's because you were too busy following up with these niggas." He frowned.

I wanted to say something smart to him but I couldn't because he was right. Lately my head was wrapped up in Nard and Dontae that I had neglected everything around me. I blamed me being bored and finding them both to be the only entertainment that I had to look forward to.

I had better things to do than to be chasing behind these damn kids that weren't mine. Maliah spent all her time doing that shit, but it was not about to be my life.

I began to scroll through pictures on Instagram when I remembered that Maliah didn't call me when she made it back home.

I told her to call me when she made it to Flint but I hadn't heard a word from her.

Worry began to weigh on me as I dialed her number. The phone rang before it went to her voice mail. I decided to call Shawnie to see if she had met her at the airport.

"Hello."

"Hey, it's Quita. Did you pick up Maliah at the airport I haven't talked to her since she left here?" I asked her with concern

"Yea she went to the gas station. She was pissed she ran into Case with Bridgette at a restaurant." She told me

"What? Case was back home with Bridgette?" I asked in shock. I was not expecting for her to tell me that.

"Yes, girl he was with her, but she went to the gas station about an hour ago now that I think about it."

"An hour ago? Who did she go with?" I questioned her.

"She took my car and went by herself." Shawnie said with anxiety in her voice.

"Shawnie, go look for her! She's not answering her phone and you know she's not safe there that's why I didn't want her fuckin going there in the first place!" I yelled.

If something happened to my sister I was going to Flint to cause a riot. My heart felt heavy letting me know that something was not right. I had to talk to Maliah, I wouldn't be able to function until I did.

I decided to call Nard to see if she was with Case or if he at least knew where she was.

"Yo'" he answered the phone.

"Hey is my sister with y'all?" I asked wasting no time

"Naw, I haven't seen her since she blew up the spot," he said.

"Well, how long ago was that? She's not answering and I'm afraid something is wrong." I whined to him.

"Have you called Case? I'm out handling some business and I'm not around anyone now."

"No I haven't called him, I'm about to and see what's going on." I said anxious to get off the phone

"Alright, hit me back and let he know what's good." He said before hanging up the phone.

I called Case before I could disconnect from Nard good. My palms were sweating; my heart was pounding and at the rate I was going I was going to have a nervous breakdown if someone didn't tell me something.

"Hello" he answered

"Case, where is Maliah? I've called Shawnie and Nard and no one seems to know where she's at." I asked with panic in my voice

"She's at Shawnie's crib." He said calmly.

"Case did you not just hear me? I just talked to Shawnie and she is not there. She said that Maliah went to the gas station over an hour ago." I explained to him with hopes that he was following what I was saying.

"Why in the fuck would she let her go to a gas station by herself?" He asked me

"I don't know but can you find her and call me back please?" I begged him

"Yeah, I'll hit you up once I get to her.

I sat on the couch attempting to call Maliah again and again but each time her phone would go to voicemail. After tiring myself out from worrying I made my way to Case's man cave and I found myself indulging in his bar. I couldn't take my nerves being on edge like this. It was too much for me to handle.

After a few shots of Cîroc, I decided to go cuddle with Aden he was the closest thing to Maliah that would bring me comfort. She had been telling me over the last few weeks that Sam and Eriq's brothers were looking for her. The more I thought about all the drama that had unfolded back home I was pissed at myself for letting her leave. If something happened to her, we were all fucked. She was all we had to depend on. I was in no position to take care of the kids I was still a big kid at heart. I made terrible decisions for myself so I was sure that I wouldn't be able to make wise decisions for the kids. I said a silent prayer as I curled up beside Aden.

Lord, I ask that you bring my sister home safe. And if she is endangered or in any pain may you deliver her and help her to think her way out of the situation to come back home.

Amen.

I went to sleep knowing that I was going to wake up to a bunch of texts from her, and her being pissed at me for calling around looking for her. I also knew that in the morning I was going to be past this scary ass feeling.

Chapter 19: Case

I couldn't believe Shawnie allowed Maliah to go somewhere by herself. She was too busy entertaining that bum ass nigga at her house to use her brain.

I banged on her front door not caring how much noise I was making. She finally answered the door looking like a sad puppy.

"Did Maliah make it back here?"

She shook her head no.

"Have you gone to the gas station that she said she was going to?" I continued to interrogate her.

"No Case, she took my car and I don't have a way anywhere to look." She confessed.

"You up in here laid up with this broke ass nigga and he don't even have a car?" I looked at her disgusted.

"Man come on, put yo' shit on and come with me so we can go find her." I said annoyed.

I didn't know why I gave Maliah a pass to leave my sight after she left the restaurant.

Shawnie moved quickly to the car as we hauled off to the gas station. I couldn't believe that I was out looking for my girl like a mad man. If only she wasn't so hard headed and stubborn she would be safe and sound right now back at home.

We pulled into a nearby gas station but there were no signs of her. Trying not to waste any time we had left I drove a few blocks up the street to another nearby gas station. Police cars and a large crowd surrounded the gas station. The officers were questioning people about something. My heart dropped down to the pit of my stomach as it began to get queasy. I gripped the steering wheel tight self-consciously. I sat there for a minute to gather my thoughts. I was nervous to face what news that I would possibly receive if I got the car. Shawnie didn't hesitate to hop out of the car to see what was going on. I instantly lost it when Shawnie pointed to the direction of her car that was empty and Maliah was nowhere to be found.

"Where is she!!" Shawnie screamed at the officer.

"Ma'am I need for you to step back over there please." The cop asked her.

"My girlfriend was driving that car I need to know where she's at." I told him

"Sir we are unsure, there was no one in the car when we arrived. Witnesses say they say a young lady running from a guy." He informed

My head began to spin in circles as I stood there trying to process what I was being told.

"What witnesses? Which way did they go?" I asked frantically

"We aren't sure we are trying to investigate. What is your name and number we will contact you when we have further details?" I walked back toward my car ignoring the cop.

"Let's go!" I yelled at Shawnie who was crying so hard that strangers were walking up to her trying to console her.

"NOW!!!" I yelled at her louder

I was pissed that she was careless enough to let her leave by herself. Maliah didn't think the streets were real, but Shawnie knew.

She was had made it to the car with a second to spare before I pulled off and left her ass. I drove full speed to her house to house to drop her off.

"I want to help you look for her, I need to know that she is okay Case." She sobbed

"Get out of my car yo' ass should have been this concerned when you let her leave by herself." I retorted

"Fuck you, don't blame me because I let a grown woman make a run to the store by herself. The real issue here is the fact that she wasn't safe going because of the bullshit you've been bringing to her life for your own selfish ass reasons, and now my friend is out there with the fuckin sharks." She cried

"Get the fuck out" I said out of anger. Shawnie was right I shouldn't have been mad at her. It wasn't her fault Maliah into all this bullshit, but regardless of how right she was *I* needed to feel less guilt as possible so that I could keep my mind clear and bring her back to safety.

Shawnie got out of the car and I peeled off with nothing but murder in my mind.

I noticed that Nard had been blowing my phone up. It clicked that Marquita had called him and he had no idea if I was missing with Maliah.

"Nigga, where the fuck are you? I've been callin you!" He snapped as soon as I answered the phone.

"Maliah has been kidnapped, meet me on the block." I mumbled before hanging up.

No matter how many positive thoughts I was trying to think my mind kept converting back to those niggas killing her. I would die if she died behind some shit she had no parts on.

I pulled up to the block and there was Nard, PJ and another nigga name Shuck that we messed with from time to time. It bothered me that he was there because I didn't trust him enough to have him in on helping me find Maliah. As far as I was concerned all these niggas were suspect.

"Aye, word is that it was Sam that she met up with at the gas station." Shuck said as I approached them

"How do you know?" I asked

"A bitch that I always serve was riding past the gas station when it happened told me." He stated

"Where do the nigga Sam live at?" Nard asked PJ and Shuck

"He used to live on Griggs but I don't know about now." PJ said

"Y'all niggas ain't useful, you fuckin live in this hood! Where the fuck does his mama, kids, bitch live at!!?" Nard asked getting annoyed.

"His mama live on Carpenter Road." Shuck spoke

"Well lead me to me her muthafuckin house then." He said walking to his car

Shuck began to follow Nard to his car.

"No, nigga you ain't riding with me. I'll follow you there." Nard spat

Shuck was a short chubby nigga, so when he swelled his chest up wanting to say something slick Nard laughed at him.

"Nigga, you better let that air out and lead me where to fuckin go." Nard threatened him

Shuck did just that, he took a deep breath and walked over to his own car. PJ tried to slide off back to his house that was across the street.

"Where in the fuck are you going?" I asked PJ

"Ain't no going home nigga, you not about to sit here and listen to what the fuck is going on and then duck off at home until the smoke clears" Nard added

PJ was never known to get down when necessary. He was the funny nigga in the hood, that everyone gravitated to. Tonight, he fucked up for being out when some shit as real as Maliah going missing had taken place.

"I'm taken it in tonight, Case I want you to find yo girl but I ain't down for the streets tonight." He admitted

I could respect anyone who was honest enough to let it be known that they were down to ride. The nervous a person was when it came to getting into some real shit increased the chances of them being the first to snitch if the situation presented itself. I was straight on either of these niggas rolling with us.

"I knew y'all were some bitches." Nard said to both PJ and Shuck

"I'on know who this nigga is or think he is but you not coming through my hood with all this disrespect" PJ spoke up

Nard began to laugh at PJ just as he had done with Shuck.

"It ain't no going home nigga. You're either rollin with us or you're dying in these streets. That's not a threat that's just me letting you know your plans for the night." Nard told PJ while staring him down

"All y'all need to chill the fuck out. I need to find Maliah so I ain't got time for all this female shit y'all all got going on. If these niggas ain't coming fine but I gotta find her." I said getting in the passenger's seat of Nard's car.

Nard stood there looking at the both of them wanting to do more in terms of probably killing them but he knew this wasn't the time nor the place for that.

"I ain't never say I wasn't down to go but you need to learn some respect" Shuck said with a trembling voice to Nard.

Without any further words, we all departed separate ways. PJ went to his house, Shuck got in his car and Nard and I got in his and followed Shuck as he led us to Sam's mother's house.

The feeling that I was experiencing was the same one I got when Bridgette took Cailey from me but worst. At least I knew that Cailey wasn't harmed because no matter how crazy Bridgette was she wouldn't physically hurt our daughter. I couldn't say that Maliah was safe right now and me finding her alive was necessary.

"I don't trust this fat ass nigga." Nard said to me

"Neither do I but what choice do we have but to let him help? I don't know shit about these niggas and our leads are dead without his help for now." I tried to get him to understand.

We followed him for over a half an hour before we pulled up in front of a bungalow house. We both got out of the car and walked over to Shuck's Chrysler 300.

"Yo whose crib is this?" I asked him unsure of where he had just led us to.

"It's they mama's house." I examined the outside of the house and it looked to be empty.

I pulled my gun off my waist and aimed it at Shucks head. He immediately began to tremble and sweat.

"What the fuck are you doing man? You asked me to lead you here and I did. That's his mama's house." He pleaded

"Go knock on the muthafuckin door then." Nard instructed

Shuck stood up straight and walked fast as he could up to the front door. He knocked three times on the door before an older lady answered. Nard and I stood on the side of the porch until the lady was comfortable in her conversation with Shuck. She knew who he was and was telling him that she hadn't seen Sam all day.

We creeped up on the porch and rushed inside of her house. Nard put the lady in a choke hold and had a gun aimed at her head.

"Who else is in here?" I asked her

"My gran...grandchildren are sleeping, please don't hurt them. Take me but please don't hurt them. I don't have no money in the house." She cried out.

I walked through the house slowly with my gun drawn. Nard and Shuck stayed behind in the living room with Sam's mama.

I walked through the house until I walked into a room of 3 sleeping kids all at least under the age of 3. The sense of guilt took over me immediately. All I could think about was my kids back in Boston and the idea of some niggas invading my house with them in it. I had to get Maliah home and I was willing to do it by any means necessary. I left the room and closed the door behind me. I grabbed a nearby chair and propped it under the doorknob to lock them in.

Once I could confirm the house was all clearing I met back up with everyone in the living room. When I walked into the room Nard had the woman and Shuck's mouth leaking with blood.

I didn't say anything to him but I gave him my *what the fuck* look. I knew that he wouldn't be able to handle just having the damn lady just sit there, his ass had to torture.

"Tell him why you just told me." Nard said to the woman

"You boys aren't nothing but trouble like your mama. I didn't want any of boys to be running around with y'all. I done lost my baby boy Eriq and I'm not losing anymore. I won't tell y'all where my son's live at." She refused

"I didn't ask you none of that shit you're talking. Tell him what the fuck you just told me or you're going to need a hip replacement." Nard threatened

"I said y'all all out here killing each other and acting crazy when you're all just a bunch of dumb asses in Joann and Gino's game. I've been seeing you Shuck riding around in the car with her like a little flunky, with yo stupid ass." She said before spitting blood from her mouth.

I looked at Nard with confusion. Why in the fuck was Shuck riding around with my mama. He sat in a chair with a look of shock on his face. He wasn't expecting her to call him out on shit. He was a stupid ass just like she said. Didn't he know that old people was the fuckin noisiest muthafuckas ever especially when it came to what was going on in their hood.

"I don't know what the fuck she is talking about man. I don't have a reason to be around Mrs. Rice." He lied with fear in his eyes.

I had known this nigga for years and never known him to work for my mama, say hi to her, or shit else.

"I have no reason to lie on you boy. You scared of these niggas, I ain't." She said

She had way more heart than this fuck boy. He was about to piss on himself the way his hands were shaking.

"What all you know Shuck? Unless you want to die in that fuckin chair I'm not going to ask you again." The anger could be heard pouring from my voice.

I was outraged that my mama was such a fuckin snake. She slithered around the hood and had her name in all kinds of shit. I was in the dark for so many years and it took me to get in a relationship with Maliah for all her skeletons to start falling out of the closet.

"I don't know shit! I ain't lying...."

POW POW POW

Before Shuck could finish his statement, Nard shot him in the head twice and Sam's mama in the head once piercing her between her eyes.

Without having to think twice I left out of the house with Nard right behind me.

"Why in the fuck would you shoot him before we got any more information out of him?" I fumed

It wasn't a part of the plan to kill him, not at this point. We left there knowing just as much information as we started with.

Rather than answer me Nard murmured "PJ has to go. I want playing about the options I gave him"

"What the fuck does PJ have to do with you taking it upon yourself to kill them?" I questioned

"The nigga knew we were there, I'm not risking the nigga snitching when the bodies come up! We got more than enough info out of the both.... ya mama is the issue. Everyone gone end up booked because the bitch is acting off her emotions rather than the code." He predicted

I didn't care what the fuck he was talking about killing my own mother was not happening no matter what she had done. I looked at Nard like had lost his mind.

"Do you hear yourself now?" I asked

"I hear myself nigga, do you not hear what all is going on right now. Yo' mama is ruining your fuckin life and you letting all this shit slide. Once a muthafucka shows me they aren't trustworthy they're dead and that goes for anybody. Give me the word and I'll light fire to her ass." He said with sincerity dripping from his voice.

Nard swerved in and out of traffic back in route to my mama's house. He called someone to take care of PJ during driving.

I was looking forward to confronting my mama but not with Nard with me. I knew what my brother was capable of and the last thing I wanted this to turn into a blood bath when I could handle my mama on my own without his interception.

I opened the door with the spare key I had. The house was dark and quiet without a soul in sight. She wasn't here, now I had to go out and hunt her ass down. Just as I was leaving out to go to back to the car where Nard was waiting Bridgette came walking down the stairs.

"Before you say some foul shit Case I just want to talk." She said defensive

"Why are you here? You can go back to wherever the fuck you were when you took Cailey." I snapped

"I came here to tell you that I was sorry, you left me Case. You left me for someone else I acted out on impulse and I'm sorry." She cried

"It's cool now I got my baby back, but you can go. You don't need to be here. There is no point." I said letting up on my tone.

She began to walk closer to me, and once she was in my comfort zone she stopped.

"Case, I don't want to leave I really want us to be together and it's not much of an option for me to go on like this if I can't have you." She continued to cry.

I didn't have the time or the patience for this shit. I had Maliah out there somewhere possibly being harmed, my own mother was looking like an enemy, and then I had this crazy ass bitch slowing me down for getting things done.

"I just told you we done. You have our daughter who needs you and yo' ass is in here talking crazy." I turned my back to walk away from her but before I could get to the door I heard a gun cock. I froze standing there. I came too far in life to be taken out by my crazy ass baby mama.

"Don't turn around Case, I'm asking you from the bottom of my heart to be with me and Cailey." Her voice was trembling and shaking.

"Bridgette put the gun down before Cailey is left out of here with no parents." I tried to rationalize with her.

"She won't be left without both parents, I love you and I would never hurt you." She said crying harder and louder.

I turned around slowly to face her, to see that she was holding a gun to her own temple.

"Bridgette, what are you doing right now? This shit isn't that serious. Put the gun down now." I said in the calmest tone that I could find under the circumstances.

I couldn't believe what I was seeing. She was off on the deep end more than what I thought. I would have never imagined that it would come to this.

"Stop telling me what's serious and what's not. That's the problem you aren't taking me serious. You didn't take our family serious, the love I have for you and I'm tired of living like this Case."

She was jamming the gun closer to her head and all I could think was, God don't let her take her own life, especially in front of me.

"I loved you Case I really did...I didn't want it to happen like this." She uttered to me

POW

One single shot to her head and she hit the floor with brains splattered on the floor and wall

"NO!! What the fuck!" I yelled kneeling down to my knees

I had been through a massacre within the last 24 hours of being home, and now had to witness my daughter's mama kill herself.

I sat on the floor for what felt like forever in a state of shock. I wanted her to get up and tell me that this was a joke and she wasn't that fuckin crazy. How would I tell my daughter this story when she grew up? Is the question I kept asking myself.

Nard came through the front door and found me sitting there fucked up over what I had just witnessed and Bridgette's lifeless body lying there.

"What happened bro??" He asked with confusion

I couldn't find the words to answer him. I just began to shake my head still in disbelief. It didn't take Nard long to figure it out. By killing being his profession he could clearly see that she had killed herself.

"Damn man…. come on bro we gotta get out of here." He grabbed my hand to help lift me off the floor.

"Naw, I can't leave. I'll wait for the ambulance. You go…go find Maliah. I need you to bring her back safe to me man." I told him in a daze.

"Alright bro, I got you. I'm gone find her for you." He said nodding his head

I was hurt in a way I didn't think that I could hurt. Bridgette and I had a ton of differences but I didn't want this for her. She was selfish as hell but tonight she showed me just how selfish she was.

"This is so fucked up." I mumbled

I didn't think I was coming back home to say "rest in peace to Bridgette" shit was getting out of control

Chapter 20: Maliah

As I sat on the floor in the dark foul smelling basement I began to think about if I would ever see the kids again. I thought about what decisions I had made in my life that led me to where I was in this moment. I even began to feel like I was going to die here and no one would find me for years.

Mrs. Rice was a monster in disguise. She was a woman who would kill, lie, manipulate and cross anyone to get to where she desired to be. It was sickening the fact that I was in this predicament because of her. I had a feeling that Casey would come and save me but after seeing the sunlight peek through the basement windows I was beginning to feel hopeless. Between my stomach growling and the stench that I smelled from the dead bodies I knew that it was only a matter of time before I passed out.

I had to think of something fast if I wanted to get out of this alive. I had no idea if she would be back to finish me off. It was no telling how this would end with the ball in her court. As the light shined through the window I could have a better view of my surroundings. My hands and feet wear tied up with rope. I pressed my back up against the wall as firmly as I could so that I could try to stand up on my feet.

After trying this for longer than I planned I accepted that it was a failed idea. I began to look around again and I spotted a piece of glass on the other side of the room. I lay on my side and began to shift my body toward the other side of the room. I had to take multiple breaks because it was a workout trying to get around without using my hands or feet as stability.

It felt like forever before I finally made it over but once I did make it to the glass I realized that this would now be the hard part. I used the tips of my fingers to prop the glass between my feet so that I could saw the rope off my hands. The rope was very thick so I had to prepare myself mentally for the challenge. I repeated to myself over and over that I could do it.

I was going to kill Mrs. Rice when I made it out. That was my mission. She had caused me more agony in this short amount of time than I deserved in a lifetime.

I continued until I felt restless. I had to keep going because I knew once I stopped it would be hard to gain the momentum back with the little energy I had to work with.

Tears began to form in my eyes. *You don't have time to bitch up now this is life or death.* I said to myself. *Stay strong, you can do this.*

I had never had as much relief as I did when the rope broke. I wasted no time untying my feet. I stood up to get the gun that was on the floor by Sam's hand. I had no idea where I was as at but I was determined to find my way to safety.

I reached the top of the stairs with one shoe on, ripped clothing, and bruised wrists. I opened the side door and stepped out with the gun drawn.

I was in an abandoned neighborhood with only two other houses on the block. I paced quickly up the street refusing to stop at those houses because I had no idea who resided in them. For all I knew it could have been workers that worked for Casey's family. I didn't know where I was going or who I could call. The only person I trusted at this point was my sister and she was all the way in Massachusetts. I had an ill thought that Shawnie had me set up and told Sam that I was headed to the gas station. I had been befriended so much that it all made perfect sense to me.

I walked until I was standing in front of a liquor store. It was now broad daylight, and I was tired not to mention hungry. Two teen girls walked out of the store together.

"Excuse me, do you have a phone I can use please?" I asked

The both of them looked at me like I had lost my mind. I looked like an addict from my appearance so their reactions did not offend me. One of the girls reached in her pocket to retrieve her phone and she slowly extended her hand to give me the phone.

I called my sister to let her know that I was okay. I could only imagine how scared and worried she was.

"Hello?" She answered

"Quita, it's me Maliah. I want you to know that I'm fine." I whispered not wanting the two girls to hear me.

"Oh my God, where have you been??? We have been worried sick about you!" She shouted in the phone

"It's a long story I'll tell you later. Please don't call Casey and tell him you talked to me. I will find a way back there soon." I told her before hanging up.

I thanked the girl and gave her back her phone.

I still had to figure out how I was going to get back to my family with no ID, no money, or anything else. My purse was left in Shawnie's car when they abducted me.

Fuck. I thought to myself

I began to walk again careful not to step on any glass on the sidewalks since I only had on one shoe. I made it my business to only trail side streets because I didn't want to be spotted walking down the busier ones.

"Aye Maliah!" Some big bearded guy called out to me off a nearby porch.

I didn't recognize him from anywhere so I ignored him like that wasn't my name.

"Come here!!" He yelled louder. I began to walk faster conscious of the gun I was still carrying on my hip and under my shirt.

I turned around and watched him walk off his porch and two other guys came from inside of the house to follow him. They began to walk in my direction and I took off running full speed refusing to be placed in the same situation that I had just gotten myself out of.

One of them began to chase me. I pulled the gun off my hip and began to shoot at him as I ran. After one shot fired the gun stopped shooting. I missed him by long shot. I pulled the hammer of the gun back and tried to shoot again but the gun was jammed. I didn't know anything about how to operate one and me shooting at him only made him angrier.

He finally caught up to me and tackled me to the ground. I fought him with everything I had in me. He wasn't big at all, standing only at about 5'5. I swung on him and my fist connected with his jaw. He grabbed my hand and pinned my arms down. I kicked him as hard as I could in his stomach. He let my arms go and folded, but by this time the other two had caught with us. They both were laughing and the ass kicking I had given him.

"Why you let her fuck you up like that?" The bearded one asked him still laughing hysterically

He was sprawled across the grass in pain, and didn't even bother to answer him.

He stood me up asked me where I was at. I recognized Antoine now that he was close. He was often around Casey when we first met.

"Yo', we've been looking everywhere for you. Where were you at? What all you've been through?" He asked.

I know I looked just like what I had been through.

"Casey's mama had me in a fuckin basement." I admitted

Antoine looked at me like he didn't hear me correctly.

"What?" He asked

"You heard me the bitch was a part of me being kidnapped." I repeated

Antoine looked at the man with the beard and shook his head

The guy I beat up stood up and stormed passed us back to the house.

"I'm sorry." I apologized to him

"Fuck you." He spat causing us to laugh.

"Damn that's fucked up. I didn't think that she was cut like that. Come down to the crib and get you something to eat." Antoine offered

I wanted to decline but it wasn't like I had anywhere to go. I needed water and food soon or otherwise I was on my way to collapsing so I followed the both toward the house.

"Please don't call Case and tell him y'all found me." I pleaded

"Now you know we can't give you word on that, he's going crazy looking for you. Why wouldn't you want him to know that you're safe?" Antoine questioned me

"I need away from him and his family. I just need to eat and I'm out." I told him

"Alright you a grown woman, if you don't want me to call him I won't." He confirmed.

I walked into the house and sat down on a nearby couch.

"Yo' Ramsey grab her something to eat." The guy with the beard said to a female that was sitting on a chair in the living room.

With an attitude, she stood up and went to the kitchen. The way she was acting I didn't want to eat shit she was preparing.

"Just show me where the kitchen is I'll get my own." I protested

"Girl you something else." He said laughing

"Naw, I'm serious, I don't want her making shit for me." I frowned

"The kitchen is straight back to the right." He pointed toward the back of the house.

I went into the kitchen to make me a sandwich, and grab a glass of water.

"Who are you?" Ramsey asked me as she walked into the kitchen.

"Why does that matter? I won't be long... don't worry." I said dismissing her

"I'm not worried I want to know who are you, you're in my mama's house." She was snaking her neck with her hand on her hip. After all that I had been this girl had no idea that I was liable to snap her neck.

I smiled politely at her and said "My name is Maliah" before walking out of the kitchen back into the living room.

The plate that I was carrying damn there fell out of my hand when I got back to the living room. Nard was standing in the door way looking at me at me like he always did which was like a hawk staring down at a predator.

He nodded his head for me to go back into the kitchen without saying a word.

I followed his command and went back into the kitchen. I was glad that little miss attitude Ramsey was still in the kitchen because maybe with her there he wouldn't be on no bullshit.

"I need this kitchen." He told her

Without any of the attitude she had given me she scurried out the kitchen as fast as she could.

"Where were you?" He asked sitting at the kitchen table

"In an abandon house." I replied as I bit into my sandwich

"How did you get there?" He was trying to piece together the scenario.

"Sam kidnapped me and took me there, yo' mama killed Sam then the bitch and a fat nigga left me down there to rot." I cringed at the memory.

"Say what?" He asked in bewilderment

I repeated everything that happened the night before leaving out any details. Nard gave me a picture of the nigga that was with her the night she left me and the basement and I confirmed that it was a nigga name Chubb's.

"Look it's a car outside and here is some money for you to make your way back to the kids. My suggestion to you is to go there and find some place to relocate y'all ASAP." Nard slid me a wad of money across the table.

I wasn't sure exactly what he was insinuating for me to do, especially without him calling Casey first.

"I second handily know you've been through some shit being with my brother and at some point, you need to walk away and get yo' shit together."

"Where is Case right now? Why isn't he here with you looking for me?" My heart began to thump hard in my chest thinkin' that something happened to him.

"He was with me but...."

"But what Nard?" Tears fell from my eyes without my permission.

"He is tied up...Bridgette killed herself today in front of him." He whispered

My eyes stretched out of my socket at the news he delivered to me. I didn't want to believe what I was hearing.

"Nard, are you serious right now?" Tears began to flow heavier down my face. I couldn't stand the girl but to hear that she took her own life over a man was devastating. It wasn't that much love in world that I would take myself from my son or siblings.

He nodded his head yes to indicate that he was telling me the truth and it wasn't a joke.

"That's so fucked up. When I get back to the kids I can't leave without him knowing, because I'll have Cailey."

We both sat there thinking for a minute.

"Come ride with me." He said breaking our thoughts from running deep.

I felt like a fool walking around looking crazy. Nard must have been reading my mind because after me riding around in the car with him he went to a close retail store and parked in the parking lot.

"What are your sizes? You looked fucked up right now man."

"Thanks for reminding me. Get me a small size, seven in pants and my shoe size is a five." I said rolling my eyes at him.

He got out of the car and I sat there wondering where he was getting ready to take me. I didn't trust Nard before, but I was beginning to feel like he was the only trustworthy person in their family and that's why he didn't mess around too much with the rest of them. His demeanor was enough to piss anyone off, but what you did have to respect about him was his realness. You were always aware of how he felt about you, and where you stood with him.

Nard came back out of the store twenty minutes later with bags in tow.

"Here" He handed over the bag.

"Thanks" I need to go someplace to shower and change.

"Yea, cuz you smell like a damn basement," he said laughing

"Fuck you." I laughed with him

"I think I need to call Casey and let him know I'm fine. He is going through a lot right now and I he has to know I'm good." The guilt of not telling him was starting to wear on me. The idea of running off and not telling him shit sounded amazing, but every time I seemed to get the confidence and urge to pull away from him some tragic shit would happen and put us right back together. I missed the kids and I needed to get back home to them.

Just as I was starting to warm up to the idea of Nard being an okay person he placed his hand on my thigh. Before any other emotion could overcome my body, I had a sense of disappointment. I was disappointed for many reasons one was the fact that my sister was madly in love with this nigga, and the fact that no one in Casey's family had an ounce of loyalty instilled within them. They was all a bunch of selfish ass people who only cared about themselves. I removed his hand off my thigh and placed it back toward his own body.

"Don't put your hands on me. Did you miss the memo that I was with your brother, you've slept with my little sister or that I just escaped a fuckin kidnapping? Your integrity level is really that low?" I wanted to belittle him as much as possible. This type of behavior was unacceptable on so many levels that he should have felt an inch tall.

He sat there quietly before saying a word out his mouth although there wasn't much that he could say.

"I don't know what just came over me, like for real. I like yo' sister and I never want to hurt my brother." He said sounding fucked up by his own actions.

"Obviously, you don't because you don't do what you just did if any of that mattered to you. It doesn't matter though, forget it happened and let's go. I don't partake in foul play." I was annoyed and pissed off.

"Seriously I don't know why, I wanted you from the day I met you at the airport. But I knew that my brother ain't into sharing like I am." He laughed while pulling off.

"Nigga please, rather he was or wasn't I would never fuck with two brothers the thought of it was sickening to me although I knew a ton of females that would. I'm straight on it." I confessed offended at the idea

Nard gave me his phone to call him Casey. I took a deep breath before calling his phone.

"Yo' bro, what's the word?" Casey asked into the phone

"It's me Casey…. I'm fine Nard is taking me somewhere now to change my clothes." My voice cracked as my voice trembled. I had no idea why I was shaking but I was. It could have been the fact that I thought I would never see his face or hear his voice again.

"Baby…. I'm so happy to hear your voice. What happened to you? Where is, Nard taking you? Put him on the phone." I didn't know rather to answer his questions or hand the phone back over to Nard. I decided to give the phone back to Nard and let him handle the call. Casey would go from calm to crazy in 0 seconds and I wasn't mentally stable to handle him.

It felt good to talk to him considering the situation his own mama put us in. Nard gave him the address to where we were going.

I didn't want to tell Casey what his mama had done. I just wanted to clip the bitch, and not hurt him with the story behind what happened to me.

We got to an apartment building and pulled around to the back door. Get out and go into apartment 206.

"What? You not going in?" No I got shit to take care of, I got to get back home in a few hours. Case is on his way.

"But how will I get in? Is the door unlocked?" I was apprehensive about going into a strange apartment that I had never been to, or know who it belonged to.

"You are good. Case will be here any second. Trust me."

I looked at him and sighed, because the bottom line was he was getting ready to leave rather I trusted what he was telling me or not; That's just what it was.

Before I could get the door closed good Nard was gone.

I entered the apartment building and walked up one flight of stairs to the second floor to find apartment 206.

Once I was standing in front of the apartment door I didn't know what I was about to walk into. I opened the door and walked inside. The inside was nice and empty. The only thing that occupied it was a futon and small coffee table. I locked the door behind me and walked around to make sure that I was the only one present in the apartment. After confirming that no one was there besides me I took a steaming hot shower. I could feel the stress roll from off my body under the water. I cried under the shower head and it felt good to cleanse. A thought crossed my mind to go home and take the kids and go like Nard suggested.

Casey was selfish enough to keep me around no matter how much agony that I endured so that he wouldn't have to live without me. I wanted to take Cailey with me because I could only imagine him being a single dad. The thought of that along sent my heart out to Cailey.

As I got out of the shower and grabbed a towel Case opened the door. I didn't know how to process the emotions that I was feeling. I was happy to see him, but in the same token I wanted to run far from him and never look back.

"Baby." He murmured hugging me. He hugged me so tight I thought that I was going to suffocate.

"You don't know how much it means to me to just hug you right now." He said holding my body.

"I understand, it was a scary feeling. I was kidnapped and I was so afraid Casey." I instantly broke down. I was being tough in front of Antoine, Nard and all the others that I had to face. But I knew with Casey I could let it all out. My heart relied on him to tell me everything would be okay, no matter what my mind was telling me.

"I know sweetheart. You don't have to relive it. I already heard exactly what happened and rest assured it will be handled."

When he said that I knew he meant just what he was saying. There was never a time when he told me that something would be taken care of and it wasn't.

"I want you to take the kids Maliah. Take some money and go. I'm not good for y'all right now. Everything is crumbling and it's still work to be done. I feel like shit for all of what's been going on with you. I need you to take all the kids and go for a while. If you must take a nanny with you do so that way you don't have too much on you by yourself, but either way you have to go baby……. please." He begged me

Tears burned in my eyes because I didn't have a choice but to go. Everything that he was saying was right, I couldn't take anymore and I was not willing to place myself in a situation to get hurt again. I held out my arms to hug him. I wanted to be within his embrace after experiencing a life or death encounter. It felt unreal standing there listening to him talk to me after what I had been through.

He wrapped his arms around me and held on to me tight. For some reason, it felt like he was going to disappear. This hug felt like it would be our last hug and the thought of that scared me shitless.

"Casey I'm scared." I mumbled into the crook of his neck.

"You'll be good, I promise you and I'm just a call away if you need me for anything."

I went in to kiss his lips and when I did the kiss felt lifeless. It was unlike any kiss we had ever had. Everything was empty. I reached down to attempt to unbuckle his belt and he stopped me.

"It's a red Jeep outside for you to take. He handed me an envelope filled with cash, my driver's license, and an airline ticket to Boston.

"How did you get my license?" I asked thumbing through the envelope.

"Out of Shawnie's car. Get to the airport before you miss your flight." The look in his eyes was cold. The warmth his eyes once gave off was now gone.

"Bye Casey." I hugged him again.

He didn't reply to me and he opened the door for me to leave.

I was devastated the entire flight back to Boston. There was an uneasy feeling that sat in my stomach. Something was not right, I felt like bad luck was right around the corner.

I don't know if I just said my final goodbye to Casey.

Chapter 21: Marquita

After talking to my sister I was relief that she was okay. Nard called me late last night to inform me that she was on her way back to us and to pack up our things because we would be relocating yet again. I was going to visit Dontae today to let him know that I would be leaving. I didn't want to break things off with him so I had hopes that wherever we were going wouldn't be too far of a distance from him.

I had a heart to heart reality check with myself to call off anything that I had felt for Nard because I didn't want to put myself through hell trying to make something work that I knew never would. As much as he texted me and told me that he *liked* me I knew that nothing more than that would come from it. The difference in the relationship that I had with him and the one I had with Dontae was that Dontae and I were becoming friends. He took the time out to ask what it was that I was about and what my interest were. When I was with Nard it was always his way or no way, and that had become exhausting for me.

I brushed my long hair while staring at my reflection in the bathroom mirror. I was a spitting image of my mama before she was hooked on drugs. Lately it had been heavily on my mind how different our lives would be now if my mama was still alive. I often wondered *would we still be back in Flint; would she have stayed clean of drugs?*

I sprayed my sisters COCO Chanel perfume on my wrist, before I did one final double take in the mirror. Dontae's dad and sister would be home for dinner and I didn't want their first impression of me to be a bad one. I didn't need some snotty rich people looking down on me for liking Dontae. After confirming with Jaylen and Ms. James what time I was coming back I headed out to the car to meet him at his house.

My stomach had a million butterflies as I arrived closer to his house. I was more nervous about telling him that I had to move with little explanation. Unfortunately, I couldn't go into major details on why I had to go and that was the part that sucked the most. As I drove through the gate to follow the path that led to Dontae's house I contemplated on turning around to go back home. My phone vibrating distracted me from backing out of my plans for the night.

"Hello."

"Are you almost here? My fam is waiting to meet you." Dontae asked impatiently

"Yea I'm actually outside, if you want to meet me at the door." I told him

There was no turning back now. I was now in front of his house parking the car. He stood in the doorway awaiting me to get out of the car.

The smile he gave me broke my heart because I was going to miss it. The way he smiled at me always managed to melt my soul. I smiled back weakly at him.

"I thought you had changed your mind, how long it was taking you to get here." He chuckled

If only he knew that I was so close to not bringing my ass here.

I walked hand and hand with him down the hallway until I reached the kitchen.

My eyes expanded out of my head as I watched Aja tossing a salad at the kitchen counter.

OMG, he's related to this bitch. I couldn't believe this shit. I knew that he looked familiar and I couldn't put my finger on it for shit and he resembled this hoe. So many thoughts ran through my mind. We could never work with her being his sister. I worried that she was getting ready to tell him about Nard and me. I had never mentioned Nard to Dontae. It wasn't much to tell him. Dontae and I weren't in a serious relationship nor were we fucking but for some reason that didn't stop me from fearing her putting my business in out there.

When she looked up and saw me she immediately pushed the salad to the side. An evil smile spread across her smile. I was now for certain that it was over for with the look that she was giving me.

"Aja, this is Marquita. Marquita this is my sister Aja." Dontae said introducing us.

"Hi Marquita, I've heard so many nice things about you." She taunted

I wanted to pull him aside and tell him all there was needed to know rather than have her hold anything over my damn head. I was not about to play with her especially since I could just beat her ass and be done with it.

"Hi Aja, I actually have met her before. She is my Nard's assistant. You know Nard, right?" I asked him

He possessed a confused expression across his face and Aja had a look of defeat on her face.

"Yea…. yea I know I Nard, he's like my brother." Dontae told me.

"Yes, they are like brothers." Aja repeated smiling.

This shit was crazy, what were the odds that he had any relations with anyone that I knew.

"Hey, you must be Marquita." An older handsome man with salt and peppered color hair said to me. I assumed this to be his dad.

"Yes, I am Marquita." I smiled back at his politeness.

"I'm Don, Dontae's dad." He said holding out his hand for a handshake.

"Nice to meet you, thank you for inviting me over." I said with gratitude.

"Let's all get washed up for dinner. It smells good in here Aja boo." Don said complimenting Aja on the dinner she helped to prepare

The entire time during dinner I wanted to stand up and walk out of the house. I was hoping that Dontae didn't pick up on my vibe because I didn't want him to think it was anything that he had done. Aja didn't say much, instead she sat there eyeballing me and hanging on to every single word that I said. I would have rather her say something than to do the shit that she was currently doing.

"So where are you from?" Don asked me

"I'm from Flint...Flint Michigan." I told him

"Oh yea, I do a lot of business that way. What brought you all the way to Boston? You go to school here?" he questioned.

"My family relocated here for a new start, and yes I go to school here." I answered him

As we wrapped up dinner I couldn't have been more relieved that it was over with.

I followed Dontae outside to sit poolside with him. I wanted to talk to him in private about me leaving. I was going to use this time as well to tell him about Nard. I had a feeling that it was only matter of time before Aja told him and I liked him enough for him to hear it from the sources mouth.

"Thank you for a great time. Your dad seems to be really nice." I told him looking at the pool.

Just as I took a deep breath to tell him what needed to be said Aja came prancing her ass outside. It was too good to be true that I was done looking at her ass for the night.

"What y'all out here doing?" she asked sitting in a sat across from us.

Neither of us said anything back to her.

"So Marquita are you out here telling my brother how you and Nard are fucking each other?" she smirked

The nerve this bitch had. If it wasn't for me caring about hurting Dontae I would have beat the brakes off her in front of him.

I looked at Dontae and his expression told me that he needed answers.

"I was out here getting ready to tell him that as well as inform him that I will be moving from Boston this week but thank you for helping me to make the announcement this way." She didn't care that she was had hurt Dontae more than she had me.

"You shouldn't have been out here worried about what I was going to tell him you should be worried about why you allow yourself to be in an abusive relationship without even being in an actual relationship." I retorted.

I could tell that I stuck a nerve in her, because she stood up over me like she wanted to hit me. I was not going to let her catch me off guard so I stood up as well.

"Bitch, fuck you! That's why you fucking the same nigga that killed your fuckin mama you a stupid ass hoe." She spat

Her words struck me like lightening She couldn't have said that Nard killed my mama. I knew that she was pressed to try and hurt me so she was willing to say anything.

"Overdose my ass, he killed the junkie." She laughed.

I blacked out, and it no longer mattered to me that Dontae was sitting there. I grabbed her by the neck and began to choke her before slamming her feather weight body on the concrete.

Dontae attempted to pull me off her but I had a tight death grip on her hair and I was not letting go. She had crossed the line speaking on my dead mama and she was going to pay with this ass whooping that I was giving her.

"Let her hair go Marquita" I heard Dontae say.

I was still hanging on to her hair. We all stood there for what felt like forever before I finally decided to let go. I held a handful of her hair in my hand and Dontae pulled me away from her.

"Just go home, I'll call you later." He said pushing me toward the door.

I was embarrassed that the evening had gone the way it had. I had every intention on having a great night and enjoying Dontae and his family. Aja was still throwing shots at me while I was walking away to leave. She was pissed that she had just taken a major lose right at home.

I ignored her loud mouth ass and turned to face Dontae to apologize. As I turned around my heart sank to the ground because a huge lawn vase was heading in my direction full speed. I didn't have enough time to duck or move out the way. The shit was happening to fast for me to have any reaction. The vase connected with my head and I instantly hit the pavement.

I could see Dontae mouthing something to me but I couldn't hear anything that he was saying to me.

Blood ran down my forehead into my eyes. Suddenly I felt extremely tired and keeping my eyes open was now impossible. I drifted off to sleep against my will. I would have never thought that this bitch was crazy enough to try and kill me over a nigga that wasn't claiming either of us.

Chapter 22: Maliah

The moment my plane landed I took my phone out of airplane mode. My notifications began to flood my phone. I had several messages from Jaylen, and Ms. James asking me to call them immediately. I found it weird that I had none from Marquita and my mind began to think the worst.

I called Ms. James phone first to find out what the hell was going on. I stood in the middle of the airport lobby waiting impatiently for her to answer her phone.

"Maliah! Please meet me at Massachusetts General Hospital… It's Marquita she was attacked." Ms. James said breathing heavily into the phone.

"What? Who attacked her!" I yelled looking around for a rental car company. I decided that process would take too long so I walked toward an exit to flag down a taxi cab. The hospital wasn't too far from the airport.

"I don't know the full story I just got a call that she is in the hospital. Hurry up I have all of the kids with me."

I got a cab within 10 minutes of standing outside.

"Get me to the General Hospital." I told the driver.

He couldn't stop the car fast enough before I was throwing him a 50 dollar will and running out the car.

I got to the registration window, and after giving the coordinator Marquita's information I was directed to the ICU unit. My heart shattered at the sight of my sister lying in the hospital bed with bruises and cuts over her face. She had a ton of swelling in her face.

Dontae was in the waiting room with Jaylen and the kids while Ms. James and I talked to the doctor.

"Whoever did this to her wanted to hurt her bad. She has a lot of fluid within her brain tissue, which is the result of traumatic brain injury. Her vitals are weak, but the baby still seems to have a strong heartbeat and, with her being comatose right now there is a chance that she will miscarry." The doctor informed us.

"Pregnant?" Was all I could manage to say.

"Yes she's about 3 weeks pregnant." The doctor answered

I stood there trying to process all the information that was just handed to me. *Who did this? Did she know that she was pregnant? Who was the child's father Nard or Dontae?* I walked out to the lobby to question Dontae.

"What happened to her?" I demanded an answer from him

"She came over my house for dinner and her and my sister got into a fight. I just wanna know that she's good."

"Your sister? Why in the hell was she fighting your sister and who the hell is your sister? Where is she?" I was ready to put my gun to use. I didn't play about my siblings.

"I guess they had some beef over Nard but my sister is Aja, and I don't know where she's at. I wouldn't tell you if I knew but that's beside the point. Is Marquita going to be okay?" He asked getting annoyed with me

"Look, if you think your sister is going to get away with this shit you got me all fucked up. And what is this shit about her being pregnant. When was the last time you and her had sex?" I asked him uncomfortably

He began to shake his head no.

"No as in not at all?" I asked

He had a look of sadness on his face, and took a seat back down in the hospital chair.

This couldn't be. My sister was pregnant and in a coma. I thought.

I didn't want to believe that she was in this condition and not only that but pregnant. I felt bad for dropping the bomb on Dontae that she was pregnant. I needed to call Nard to see if he had heard from Aja or knew her whereabouts. That bitch was as good as dead her and Mrs. Rice I had a hit list and the both were at the top of it

"Yo' you touched down?" Nard asked me upon answering the phone

"Yea I made it. Aja attacked my sister today and she's now in critical condition. Did you know about this shit?" I felt my hands shaking just asking him about the shit.

"What in the fuck? What hospital is she at? And no, I ain't know shit about it."

"She's at the General hospital here. You need to get here ASAP to handle this situation."

"I'm about to catch the next flight out. You talked to Case?" His question made me realize that I had not heard from him since I made it back to Boston.

"No I haven't talked to him, and I honestly don't have any plans on calling him either." I was serious this time Case was no longer a part of my life and I was going to do everything in my power to make sure of it.

One of the messages that I received when I got off the plane was from Shawnie and she was telling me that Case was on his way to Chicago to be with Bridgette's mama. I know that he was carrying the burden of her taking her own life.

The truth of the matter was she was battling demons that he couldn't help her with. The girl had more issues than a little bit.

Behind me being kidnapped, all his mama's skeletons falling out of the closet and I knew it was having him losing his mind.

I took Cailey from Kayla's arms and held her close to me. I didn't know if I had the strength to take care of another child all by myself but if it was one thing that I did know I was going to try. I couldn't turn my back on her she didn't ask for none of this. Sitting there rocking her in my arms, and her smelling so pure brought tears to my eyes. Her mother didn't love her enough to make sure that she was first. She loved a selfish man more than this precious little girl. The thought of that was unbelievable to me.

I found it crazy that every time I was planning on getting away from all things associated with Casey I would get trapped to stay because of some tragedy taking place. It has never failed that I was tied to him by heart-ship and misfortune. It was the very thing that brought us together. The way things seemed it was never set up for us to live happily ever after.

I let my thoughts run freely as I sat there for hours in the hospital lobby. Ms. James had taken the kids home to feed them leaving only Dontae and me there at the hospital. Being there made me feel closer to my sister. I was afraid that if I left I would lose her forever.

"You should go home and get some sleep." Dontae suggested to me

"No, I'm not leaving her here." I mumbled

"You just look tired; I'll stay with her and keep you updated. I'm sure the other kids miss you."

"No I'm staying, you need to go home." I rolled my eyes at him

Although it was wrong of me I held him responsible for what happened to my sister. I didn't know why he didn't do more to protect her from his hating ass sister

"I guess we will both just be here then." He said looking down into his phone.

I was getting tired. I hadn't had any real rest for days. I didn't care about my own situation after hearing this news. Mrs. Rice was going to get hers that was all I sought when it came to her. She had done the unthinkable.

As I was beginning to drift into sleep Nard came walking through the hospital's double doors

He stopped walking towards me and stood there looking at Dontae. From the look on his face I could tell that he was shocked and confused to see him here. After his long dramatic pause, he continued to walk towards us.

"Yo', what you doing here bro?" He asked standing in front of Dontae.

"We were kickin' it and shit." Dontae answered

"Who? Kickin' it with who?" Nard looked back and forth between the both of us.

"Me and Marquita." He said sternly

"How long this shit been going on?" Nard snapped

Dontae remained cool and answered "Not that long... a few weeks."

Nard's hand was twitching and his face was turning red as he took a seat next to me.

"You're worried about the wrong shit, she may not make it because of your bitch and you out here questioning him." It was crazy to me how territorial niggas were.

He was sitting here pouting that her and Dontae was talking but he had a whole bitch that tried to kill my sister because of his ass.

"Dawg I don't even know why the fuck I'm here, obviously, she was choosing my lil bro." He said to me

"What you mean you don't know why you're here. My fuckin sister is struggling to keep her life and pregnant with your baby and you think you shouldn't be here?!" I felt myself getting fired up hearing him talk like this

"Pregnant? Y'all on some other shit up in here. How do you figure she's pregnant by me when my brother is sitting here in the waiting room for the same chick?" I shook my head in disbelief at his word choice.

"Naw, I ain't hit it." Dontae admitted

"You making some big assumptions, I hate this shit happened to her. And I'm here to make sure she's straight, but I don't want to hear about no baby talk, especially since I can't ask Marquita myself."

He moved over a couple of seats next to Dontae and began talking to him. They were talking so low that I couldn't hear a word either of them was saying.

All that I knew was that if they weren't handling Aja then I was she was as good as dead in these streets and my word was marked on it.

Chapter 23: Case

I sat in hotel room in downtown Chicago with my phone turned off and my mind on overdrive. I had led myself to believe that everyone around me was better off without me being around. I had thoughts of killing my own mama. I was battling the vivid memory of Bridgette killing herself in front of me. I was still fucked up of the thought of Maliah being kidnapped and the amount of killing I had partaken in within a short amount of time had me going crazy.

Bridgette's funeral was coming up in a few days and I wasn't prepared mentally to stand before her family after the incident. I told myself repeatedly that I was not to blame for what happened but it was so hard for me to believe that. The history that she and I had together ran deep and this was something that I couldn't accept.

My stomach began to rumble reminding me that I hadn't eaten anything all day. I thought about what I wanted but nothing sounded good to eat.

Fuck it I'll go grab a pizza.

I decided to walk down to the pizza spot on the corner since I didn't any patience to wait on valet to bring me my car.

Apart of me wanted to call Maliah and see where she and the kids went off to. Knowing her she probably took that money and went way over to the west coast to get away from all the bullshit that she had been through.

Regardless of where she traveled off to I know that she was somewhere thinking about me which was something that I didn't want. I wanted her mind be off me. As much as I missed and needed her to console my heavy heart and troubled mind I loved her enough to let her go. At some point as a man I had to know when to draw the line and let her experience better than what I was putting in her life. Even though none of the shit was caused by me directly it was still all stemmed from her being associated with me.

I stood impatiently inside of the pizzeria waiting for a short brown skin chick to call my number. After I ate I knew I would finally be able to get some rest. If I didn't sleep sooner than later my body was sure to shut down and I wouldn't have to worry about it.

"Hey sweetie your number is up." She said smiling at me

"Thanks." I grabbed the bag off the counter.

"Anytime baby." She said trying to shoot her shot

I was too exhausted to entertain her efforts at trying to flirt with me

"What you ordering today Roc?" She asked a fat nigga standing in the line

I went to walk out the store content that I had my food.

"Aye, I left my wallet out in the car give me a second." The fat nigga said to the waitress

The way that he looked at me didn't sit well with me and I was happy that I didn't leave without my strap on me.

I didn't know a soul from Chicago outside of Bridgette's family and this nigga didn't look familiar.

I walked slowly making sure that he stayed within my eyesight as I walked in the opposite direction of my hotel. I wasn't going to lead him to where I was laying my head at for the night.

I continued to walk and made it my business to stay amongst the busy street that I was walking down. I looked out of my peripheral and he was still sitting in his car. I was sure that my nerves were just bad from all the shit that I had been through but I couldn't be too sure and the nigga was looking at me like I had shot his mama.

As I went to walk across the street I was cut off by a Buick Supreme that came out of nowhere. The niggas had red bandanas over their mouths and covering half of their faces. Two Shot guns were pointed at me by the passenger and a nigga in the backseat.

"Oh shit." I managed to say looking at the barrel of the guns pointing directly at me.

I wasn't sure if this was karma, being at the wrong place at the wrong time or what the fuck was going on. I didn't have on anything flashy and I wasn't from here so I had no idea what these niggas motives were.

I stood there contemplating my next move when the fat nigga from the restaurant comes walking up.

"Muthafuckin Case." He said rolling a tooth pick around in his mouth.

I studied his face and I had no idea who he was. I hadn't seen him a day in my life. I would have remembered a nigga as ugly as he was.

"Yea', I know who you are nigga? Where is yo" bitch Bridgette at? That hoe thought she was going to get away with stealing money from me. If I can't catch up with her I'm going to blast yo' ass. That will hurt the bitch seeing as though how much she loved you." He said mugging me

Him mentioning the love Bridgette had for me opened the wound that I had in my heart even more. I almost forgot about the guns pointing at me until the passenger engaged the pump on the double barrel shot gun.

Beads of sweat begin to form on my forehead, because my adrenaline was pumping off the fact that I could beat his fat ass if he didn't have me targeted with a gun.

"Bridgette is dead." I mumbled

"Oh, what you killed the bitch? She dissed me for a nigga that killed her?"

This nigga was bitter, and that told me that no matter what I said he already had in his mind what he was getting ready to do. I would never fold under pressure so I was prepared to stand my ground to him rather than act like a bitch.

It was broad daylight and there were a ton of bystanders standing around us. I didn't know what Bridgette had stolen of his or told him about me but it had him highly upset that nothing mattered to him at this point but making her pay for it.

"Nigga you think you tough standing there, you think you the man and shit? I'm go tell yo' ass like I told that bitch…I'm that nigga and if the hoe is dead she'll be happy to be with yo' ass in hell. Nobody steals from me and think they can get away with it. It ain't happening."

If I was going to make one attempt at saving my life I had to do or say something fast.

"My man, I don't know what she took from you or said to you about me but it has nothing to do with me personally. I can pay you back for what she took, but she is dead so ain't no pint in trying to hurt her or make her suffer." I said pleading my case.

"Naw, you can't pay back shit. That bitch stole my pride and ego as a man. You know how much money that shit cost big dawg? You know how that feel to have a bitch show you pictures of another nigga she thinks is better than you? Nigga I run Chicago. This is my city blood." He retorted griming me up and down

This shit was all crazy to me for so many reasons. I was a long way from home, Bridgette was dead, and she was dead because I rejected her and this nigga was threatening to kill me. I was the wrong nigga for this. Shit. Out of all the shit that I had done in my life I couldn't believe that I was in this predicament because a nigga couldn't take a blow to his ego over some shit a female said to him.

I wanted to pull my pistol out but I knew I would be shot before I had a chance to if I made a sudden move. These Chicago niggas wasn't about calling anyone's bluff they were here to handle whatever it was that his fat ass told them needed to be handled

This dumb ass emotional nigga wouldn't get out of his feelings long enough to kill me and be done with it. He waited so long that police sirens could be heard in the distance. Both gun men were getting uneasy as they heard the sirens too.

Before I had a chance to process his words my body locked up as the bullets penetrated my body. The heat travel through my body from the bullets and the burning sensation was too intense for me to want to fight for my life. All my internal organs began to shut down as I struggled to gasp for air. The ambulance sirens were beginning to fade out as blood poured from my mouth and my body began to jerk uncontrollably.

I would have never imagined that I would die in the streets of Chicago with no one I knew or loved there to save me or lay beside me so I didn't have to die alone. I had so much shit that was unresolved that I still had to take care of. I guess Bridgette someway somehow still made sure that if she couldn't have me no one would.

My legacy would be left unwritten with half ass story left to be told. I had finally found something to live for a family of my own, but this was some shit that I didn't want to die for. I didn't want to die because of the love Bridgette displayed for me to the next man.

This shit couldn't be real. Was my only thought

Chapter 24: Nard

The shit Maliah told me was fucking with my mind. I was experiencing so many emotions that I wasnchapte't familiar with. I wanted to kill Aja for what she had done to Marquita. I fucked with a lot of females and she had never resorted to these types of measurements. It was like she knew before I did that Marquita would imprint on me. I couldn't deny that everything that I was against, she had me feeling indifferently about; *love* being one.

I liked her more than I liked anyone outside of my family. The thought of her being in a coma while pregnant with my child had me going crazy. I made up my mind that I was going to find Aja and she was going to pay for this shit.

I held Marquita's hand hoping that she would squeeze it and give me some sign that she was here with me. I wanted to tell her I was sorry for giving her a hard time and to ask her to forgive me for all the times that I'd hurt her feelings by telling her that she would never be my girl.

It was crazy that I even wanted to check her ass about talking to Dontae behind my back. I was annoyed that he kept randomly popping up at the hospital to check on her. If he wasn't like my little brother I probably would have whooped his ass. I could tell he was carrying around guilt on him because of this shit. But I explained to him that he couldn't control what his crazy ass sister did.

What fucked me up the most was that I already knew without a doubt the heavy consequences that's Aja was going to pay for this shit but I had to be more than ready to gear up for war because he pops was in the same profession as me. That was how I met her. He was the head nigga when it came to assassination. He retired from the Marine Corps as a gunnery Sargent. His level of expertise was solid, and his connects ran deep. With me knowing this I had to be ready always.

As a man, I couldn't turn my cheek and pretend this shit didn't happen because I was afraid of what her daddy would do. Marquita didn't deserve this shit. It wasn't her fault that Aja was an unstable bitch that didn't want to feel a sense of replacement by the next.

"She's showing signs of improvement and the baby still has a strong heart beat." The doctor said to me looking at her charts.

Hearing that news brought a smile to my face.

"That's good to know. Worst case scenario the longer she stays in a coma what are the odds of her not carrying the baby full term?"

"It's possible that a comatose woman can carry a baby full term. It is rare but it's known cases of its existing. With the progress, she's making I think that she and baby will be fine." The doctor assured me

I didn't think that I would ever be a dad and I damn sure didn't think I would have the news delivered to me this way.

When the doctor left the room I gently placed my hand on Marquita's stomach. I wanted her and the baby to make it out of this. The only problem that I had with the way things were playing out was that I was responsible for killing Eriq *and* Rose. I couldn't have a future with a woman whose mother I killed. Although it was a just a job to me at the time it came back around that I had killed my child's grandmother.

All that I could hope was that Marquita never found out that I was responsible. The only person that knew about me being the hit man behind both deaths was Aja and no matter what she and I went through that was confidential information that she wouldn't leak no matter how emotional she had become.

When I got the call from my step mama to get the job done I was on top of making it happen. She had done enough damage to the lives of my brother and me. It was time for that bitch to meet her maker. I knew that Case would never forgive me for what I was about to do but I couldn't see why he wouldn't understand.

I left the hospital to go home and prepare to go back to Michigan. I hadn't heard from Case and neither had Maliah. I told her to find a spot for her and the kids in Connecticut. I didn't want them in that house in Boston another day because Aja knew it like that back of her hand. She had been around me long enough for me to know that she could be cruel as fuck but it was only a matter of time before she came out of hiding and I would catch her.

~~~~~~~~~~~~~~

When I arrived in Michigan my gut told me to go and talk to my pops first. I didn't need his grace to do what I felt but I needed him to know that it was necessary that his wife be taken out because she could no longer be trusted and she made it very clear that it didn't matter who she crossed to get the results that she wanted out of any situation.

My dad sat in a recliner looking through his investor's magazine.

"Yo', pops how is it going?" I asked taking a seat across from him

"I'm good son, can't complain. The question is, how are you? You and your brother have been extremely messy lately." He said to me putting the magazine down

"Yea I know, and that's exactly why I am coming to you. It's been so much shit going on lately that I've been trying not to bring to you. But that wife of yours is responsible for all of it. I don't know what the fuck her problem is but she has been making life for everyone a living hell." I vented to him

"Welcome to the club she's been making mine that way for years now." He agreed

"Well, I have to tell you that she has to be handled I held out long enough because she is related to Case but the bitch is nobody to me but your wife. I have a lot of shit fuckin with me… I have a baby on the way pops and I killed the grandmother of my child because of a hit the she assigned me to." I confessed to him

"A baby on the way? You have a baby on the way? Who is the girl and who in hell was her mama?" He asked me in a state a state of shock

I went on to give him details about Marquita, and how I felt about the killing of Rose. It was therapeutic to talk to him about everything that was on my mind. The things that I was opening up to him about I wouldn't let another soul hear this side of me.

"She was so bitter about y'all being mixed up with them because so many years ago I use to mess around with Rose. This was before she got hooked on that shit. After Maliah's dad died I was there for her and I felt obligated to look out for her for so many years because it was my supply that she took her first hit from. It was even rumored around the city that her son was mine, but by then she was fucking so many other niggas I didn't even bother entertaining it." He sat in deep thought reminiscing about whatever he and Rose had in the past, and from the look in his eyes he had a lot of love for her.

That all explained why Case's mama didn't want him dealing with Maliah. She was bitter about the affair that my pops had with her mom's.

"But it's all a thing of the past you don't have to worry about her fuckin with y'all anymore, I put her ass away." He said nonchalant while picking his magazine back up

"Put her away? What you mean…she dead?" I asked with my eyebrow raised

"No she's not dead but her ass won't be back." He said nonchalant

I chuckled to myself because I envisioned him putting her in some type of underground cell like Olivia Pope's pops did her mama on the show *Scandal.*

"Don't sweat the light shit son, she will never have a way of knowing that you were responsible for what happened to her mother, because I was in agreeance to it being done. Her mother didn't serve her life any good anyway and besides you had no idea."

He was right Marquita would never know and even if she did in my mind she couldn't be mad at me because I didn't know shit.

My phone was vibrating in my pocket non-stop for the past hour and I had been ignoring it.

Whoever it was didn't leave me a message so it couldn't have been important. I thought about Marquita being in the hospital and decided to answer because it could have been pertaining to her since I had left my number with the nursing staff.

"Hello?"

"Hi is this Nard Rice speaking?" a woman asked over the phone

"Who is this?" I asked caught off guard by her using my first and last name.

"I'm Detective Melissa Fields with the Chicago Police Department. Is this Mr. Rice speaking?"

"Yea this him." I said sitting straight up so I could actively listen to her.

"Hi Mr. Rice. I am calling you in regards to Casey Miller he has been involved in a shooting. I can't disclose detailed information without properly identifying you. Are you able to come to a disclosed address within the 24 hours?" she asked

My heart stopped beating for a good 15 seconds. I knew my brother went to Chicago to help with the arrangements of Bridgette's funeral but this was unexpected.

"Yes, I can." I grabbed a piece of paper and pen to write down the information that she was giving to me. My dad listened attentively with a look of concern on his face.

After hanging up with her I told him what I had just discovered and we were on the next plane out of Michigan to Chicago.

Case being dead was something that I would not live down. He was my best friend, my only friend, my brother. My stomach was getting weak as replayed the call I received in my head.

Why in the fuck did I let him go alone? I asked myself as the plane took off

Chapter 25: Maliah

I sat on the stairs of a condo in downtown Hartford Connecticut that I had settled in. Although I had only been there for a week I was already at peace. I decided against Ms. James coming with me because Jaylen was all the help that I needed with Kayla, Aden and Cailey. It also had a lot to do with the way my trust was set up. She had done nothing to show me that she couldn't be trusted but I was more at ease knowing that I didn't have to look over my shoulder making sure she wasn't on no bullshit.

I watched Aden sliding down the stairs while laughing hysterically. I started to laugh with him. Cailey sat at the top of the stairs between Kayla and me clapping her hands and cheering Aden on. Kayla was zoned out trying to style her dolls hair after seeing it being done on YouTube. The sight before me warmed my heart and it made me realize that I had been so neglectful to them drowning in my own depression. Nothing mattered more to me than these kids and I had to keep in mind that no matter what came my way they would always be there in the end.

My phone had not rung once with a call from Nard or Casey, and I was okay with that. Nard told me that he would visit Marquita everyday while he stayed behind in Boston. I didn't have much of an option but to believe that he would. My plan was to travel back there every weekend until she was stable enough to be transported to a hospital in Connecticut.

I wanted to give Casey his space and I for damn sure needed mine after all the shit that I been through fucking around with him and his sick ass family. I knew that eventually he would come around to check up on the kids if nothing else, that I was certain of. I didn't have anyone else to talk to outside of Shawnie and she was walking around with guilt of me being kidnapped.

I told her to ignore what Casey said to her the night I went missing. She told me everything word for word that he said to her and it pissed me off that he would put that type of blame on her.

I lit a candle and placed it on my fireplace mantle and searched my playlist to listen to some Jill Scott. I began to contemplate what was for dinner when my phone began to ring.

Just as I was thinking about Shawnie she was calling me.

"Hey girl." I beamed into the phone. I was so happy to hear from her.

"Hey Honey, how are you?" she asked

"I'm good, I can't complain… even if I wanted to it wouldn't change shit." I laughed into the phone. I picked up a menu from a nearby restaurant in search of something quick that could be delivered for dinner.

"That's so good for me to hear girl. I thought that I would check in on you after hearing about what happened to Case. I was hoping that you hadn't gone off on the deep end. Is he okay now?" she asked with concern

I didn't have a clue as to what she was talking about. I hadn't gotten any news about Case and now I was anxious to know what exactly was she talking about.

"What are you talking about? What happened to him?" I asked putting the menu down and gave her my undivided attention.

"Wait…you aren't with him? I'm so sorry honey I just knew that you were with him. He was shot last week. I'm not sure what condition he's in. I barely received that info. You know that side of the family don't fuck with me like that since they said I tell you everything. Last, I heard he was in Chicago, but now I'm worried." She stated frantically

"Let me call you back Shawnie." My mind was running a million miles per hour.

"Okay please do, let me know if y'all need anything."

I hung up from her to call Nard. I was confused why he had not contacted me. I understood that we were giving each other space but this was an extreme circumstance. I called Nard twice but neither of my calls received an answer. My nerves would be on edge until l I heard from him. It bothered me that I didn't have anyone else to call to check on him. I decided to call Casey's phone but his phone went straight to voicemail just as I thought it would.

All I could do was pace my condo for hours driving myself crazy until I thought to call hospitals in the Chicago area to see if he was a patient in any of them. I called Mercy hospital and learned that he was admitted there but I couldn't get any information from them operator on his status.

Now that I knew where he was I still have no peace in not knowing if he was stable or severely hurt. It killed me that I wasn't by his side because no matter how much I knew that he wasn't any good for me I still loved him deeply. I was frustrated that I had no one to stay with the kids and I would be forced to travel with all of them in tow.

I already had the burden weighing on me with the kids asking me why all of the diminished relationships were forming from my mom, Eriq, Marquita, Ayesha, Mrs. Rice, and now Casey. Those were all people in their lives that they had personal relationships established with and I had a hard time explaining to them to where they could understand that life was taking us on a roller coaster.

The traveling arrangements for us to head to Chicago were thrown together in a short amount of time. While I was putting it all together Jaylen was helping me get everyone packed up. It felt like we were on the movie *Home Alone* with the way we were running around the condo with our heads cut off and kids everywhere. I was hoping that Aden and Cailey slept most of the flight. Once we made it to our hotel room Jaylen could sit with them while I went to the hotel room to check on Casey.

The flight there went the exact opposite of how I planned for it to go Aden and Cailey both stressed me the fuck out crying and acting crazy. When the plane landed, I knew everyone on it was ready to run up off of it the way they cut up. I had to wait another hour at the airport for my rental car and by the time we made it to the hotel we all were exhausted. I was too antsy to take a nap first., instead I took a shower and got in the car and headed straight to the hospital. I made sure to book a hotel that was close to the hospital so that I was still within reach of the kids. Jaylen had his phone and knew to call me the second he needed anything. Honestly once I knew that he was okay I would be going back home immediately there was no need for me to stick around.

"Hi I'm here for Casey Miller." I said to the registration clerk. Visiting hospitals was becoming too familiar and I didn't like it one bit.

"Casey Miller." She repeated looking at her computer monitor.

"Yes he was just removed from the ICU unit into HDU." She informed me. I didn't know if the HDU was worst that ICU but it all didn't sound good to me.

"I need for you to sign in please." She politely said as she handed me a clipboard in exchange for my driver's license.

"Okay, you're going to go through these double doors, and head straight until you reach the elevator. Take the elevator to the 4th floor and he is in room 402." She instructed

"Thank you." I couldn't wait to get to him. I was still praying that he was okay.

When I made it to his room the door was pulled up. I slowly opened and saw Nard, and a female who I had never met before sitting at his bed side. Casey was sleeping in a hospital bed and he appeared to be in bad shape.

Nard looked like he had swallowed a quarter when I came into the room.

"Why haven't you returned any of my calls? What happened to him Nard?" I asked heated.

"I didn't want you to worry, he will be okay." Nard mumbled under his breath.

"You didn't want me to worry? I began to worry when you couldn't pick up the phone to tell me he was *okay.*" I huffed rolling my eyes annoyed by his bullshit.

"Hi, I'm sorry I don't think we've met before." The girl said as she stood up to shake my hand.

I was highly upset and I was not in the mood to meet one of Nard's bitches especially when I thought he was in Boston with my sister.

"Hi. I'm Maliah." I said in a dry tone ignoring her attempt to shake my hand.

"I'm Brandy…Case's fiancé," She smiled wide still with her hand out

Before I could confirm if I heard her correctly I punched her square in her face as hard as I could and it caused her crash to the floor. Nard stood up to try and stop me from kicking her but he was a second too late because my foot connected with the same spot that my fist had just landed in on her face.

"FIANCE? WHAT THE FUCK IS GOING ON NARD? I yelled at the top of my lungs in an outrage. Casey's eyes opened and roamed the room with confusion until his eyes connected with mine. I had hot tears streaming down my face, my heart was racing, my adrenaline was pumping and most of all my heart was broken. "You ain't shit nigga, not even on your death bed! I hope you die in this muthafucka Case!" He shook his head from side unable to talk with all the tubes running down his throat. I traveled for hours with kids including *his* biological daughter for this shit. He had just laid one bitch to rest and another one had come out the wood works. This shit was too much.

The hospital security came into the room with the nurse. The bitch was lying on the floor crying and bleeding. I knew without a doubt I was about to get arrested, and have to post bond. Nard must have read what I was thinking because he came over to me so I could whisper to him where the kids were.

"What's going on?" the officer asked her

"I'm visiting my fiancé when she came into the room and just attacked me." She stated.

Hearing her call, him her *fiancé* sent me into an outrage all over again. "Just get me the fuck up out of her NOW!" I yelled to the security guard. I was too out done and as far as I was concerned Case was dead to me.

I was numb to everything at this point, no matter which way I turned I was being fucked over but this took the cake. This nigga had made a fool out of me for the last and final time. There was no more Maliah she was dead and gone to. It was time for me to going about everything Rambo style.

I looked at Case one last time and he mouthed *sorry* to me.

"You will be." I threatened him as the policeman escorted me out of the room.

The Final Installment Coming Soon...The Price of Loving a Hustla: Maliah's Revenge